LONG ROAD TO EDEN

Philip Charles Eckman

Published Independently

Copyright © 2024 Philip Charles Eckman

All rights reserved

The characters and events portrayed in this book are fictitious. Any similarity to real persons, living or dead, is coincidental and not intended by the author.

No part of this book may be reproduced, or stored in a retrieval system, or transmitted in any form or by any means, electronic, mechanical, photocopying, recording, or otherwise, without express written permission of the publisher.

ISBN-13: 979-8-33-766665-5

Cover design by: PCEckman (with AI assisted Imagery)

Printed in Canada

"To be, or not to be, that is the question."
William Shakespeare

CHAPTER 1

A thin column of smoke rising from the downtown core in the putrid afternoon…

An orange glow at its base…

Fire.

Not from a bomb this time. No explosive echo had rippled across the cityscape. Burning days are every third Sunday. Today is the first Tuesday, so no, it couldn't be that.

Is it a Molotov cocktail? Could it be a poor man's house afire, or something much bigger? A larger building. If it's The Administration on fire, then good.

"Jack Parnell…!"

Jack knows the voice well. Since childhood. He turns to see a handsome, slender man crossing the street toward him. Henry Chagall. He of the silver hair and pale blue eyes. Only fifty-nine, but since Reckoning, considered elderly. He, like Jack Parnell, now nearing his formal end of days; Eveningsong. Unless this day with the column of smoke and orange glow means the true end of days. For everyone.

Jack holds out his hand. "Henry...."

He remembers times long gone. Henry's arms embracing him. Tender kisses on his neck. Even now, Jack feels arousal as Henry clasps his hand. Even at fifty-nine, and after breaking away from him, Henry can still inspire an erection.

"It's been a long time, Jack."

They fall into silence, staring into one another's eyes, wondering if each can still trust the other. Even though they've known each other since they were eight years old and later became lovers, it's unwise to trust anyone since Reckoning.

Together, they step up to a nearby promontory overlooking the downtown area. They squint at the cloud of smoke, now dissipating; drifting on a breeze that seems to blow in from nowhere, penetrating what had been a languid afternoon. Now the sound of distant sirens, growing louder and louder. Fire engines sent to squelch the licking flames.

Henry unknots a neckerchief he wears and wipes his sweaty brow.

"It's at city core. I suppose someone hit The Administration again."

Each is silent as they gaze. It'll be over soon.

The grey...

The orange...

Efficient containment, like similar incidents before it...

Just another day.

But it's never over. The Administration will

retaliate. There'll be a sweep. Jack looks askance at Henry, wondering which side he's on, knowing full well that Henry wonders the same thing about him; that it's best to say nothing to an old lover, unhailed or well-met since Reckoning.

To give no hint.

Such tragedy that friends who, at age eight, pricked their fingertips and pressed them together to blend their blood and swore allegiance for life, could no longer be sure of one another; certain of their love, although shattered.

"Is this your neighbourhood now, Jack?"

"No...."

He holds up a canvas bag stuffed with baked goods and nods toward a squat building nearby. The smell of fresh pastry wafts through an open door into the already overheated afternoon.

"I come here for the bread. Best in the city."

He notices Henry has not taken in his words about bread, or the best bakery in the city. No. He seems focused on a different detail as he clasps Jack's hand between his; again, a fixed and intense look from his pale blue eyes.

Pained...

Searching.

"We must get together soon, Jack. It's been too long. Give me your number and I'll call you."

Jack feels the alarm in his gut; the panic felt whenever he suspects someone seeks details to add to his profile. For that reason, he avoids all social media. And for that reason, he has no cell phone or landline at home; instead, preferring public phones. Though nowadays there are so few. Still, it's futile. Facial recognition is everywhere, even in phone booths. Truth be told, he knows The Administration knows everything about him. Even the cash register at the bakery transmits the receipt for bread to big data. They catalog the number of people who prefer whole wheat to processed white flour and raisin scones instead of croissants. No matter. He still feels compelled to defy, even in small ways.

"I have no phone."

"No phone...?"

"I'll have to call *you*, Henry."

He glimpses the corners of Henry's mouth turn up; a telltale sign from days long-gone when something offside amuses him. Most often, Jack's defiance. Henry takes a pen from his shirt pocket and takes Jack's hand, holding it palm up. He inscribes a telephone number there.

"Commit it to memory. It's vital I speak to you."

With that, he strides away and disappears around a corner...

Gone.

***

A cramped room...
Dingy, peeling wallpaper...
Dust in the corners...
Rust...

Mould.

Jack sets down his canvas bag stuffed with bread on a rickety table. Crossing the gloomy room, he fills a kettle and places it on a solar hotplate. He stares out an open window at the street below, lost in thought. The air has grown still again, and sultry.

He'd lied, not wanting Henry to know that he lives two doors away from the bakery in two threadbare rooms above a hardware store. He doesn't want anyone to know. Only the slovenly owner of the hardware store knows for certain that someone occupies these rooms. And other denizens of the ramshackle neighbourhood who watch comings and goings. But, like Jack, have reasons to avoid association, or to draw attention to themselves.

When he agreed to rent the rooms, he supplied a false name. The property owner suspected as much. But he's greedy enough to accept a premium on rent. He went along with the ruse. So, Jack got his ragged, yet expensive rooms off-record.

Even before Reckoning, he'd started limiting his profile. He knew what was coming; that at sixty, he must accept Eveningsong; an inoffensive term for mandatory death.

Climate change has ravaged the planet, quicker than even the scientists imagined. Let alone indecisive and self-serving politicians. Also, the one-percenters who earn dividends from industries that have caused the crisis. The Youngers blame Jack's generation and all those who came before him. The revolution, or "Reckoning" was swift and decisive. To save the planet and themselves, The Youngers banded together. They organized via social media, and all over the world, the slaughter began.

The one-percenters went first. Their extreme wealth couldn't save them. With vast technical expertise, The Youngers pillaged it, transferring it into The Grand Account.

Even each nation's technological weaponry turned upon itself.

Bombs fizzled…

Armies fell…

Anarchy…

Blood.

Next to go were the infirm, disabled people, and the challenged; anyone who is a drain on scant resources with no hope of giving back.

Within only three years, the world's population decreased by twenty percent. Within the next three years, more will reach the age of Eveningsong and, coupled with a low birthrate, projections are that the population will decrease another twenty-five to thirty percent.

Then, they theorize that nature, less burdened, can return to balance. Correct itself.

The kettle whistles. Jack steeps a used tea bag and sips.

Henry had used the word vital. He'd said,

"It's *vital* I speak to you."

***

A deserted street…

Darkness between dim bluish pools of light which solar lamps cast on the sidewalk…

Sunrise is two hours off, but the air swelters…

Rancid, it stings the throat.

Jack peeks around the corner of a tumbledown building before turning onto a narrow cross street, at the end of which stands a grimy, graffiti-covered phone booth. As far as he can tell, few people use it, and no one is there now; its facial recognition lens scratched and spray-painted until The Administration replaces it. Such vandalism, one too many times, and they'll remove the phone booth all together. Then where will he go to make a call such as this? A call that Henry said was vital.

He can pinpoint the exact instant it all fell apart.

William….

But, truth-be-told, it'd started well before that: when he and Henry went from love to apathy. That moment was more difficult to pinpoint. There must've been a wrong word; a hurtful statement-of-fact. There must've been something that engendered pain, or boredom with one another's foibles, once found endearing. Something that made the most important person in their lives, now the least. On whom could he place blame? Henry? Him? Or both. Had they each arrived at an *all-roads-lead-to-Rome* revelation at the same instant? Or was there a slow, insidious erosion that went unnoticed, or even unchecked, until it was too late? Had they each heard each other's stories too many times until there was nothing more to share? To excite. It was all too long ago to fathom; the second they shattered. So long since they'd last slept in the same bed. Even longer since they'd grappled under a sweaty sheet. But time never out of mind. Time for Jack to remember what he loves about Henry. And there's so much.

Time to grieve the loss of it...

Time to grieve William.

Now, after so much has happened in the world, *to* the world, Henry used the word "vital." It was not a mistake, a lazy turn of phrase. Henry isn't one for hyperbole. He'd been the practical one in the relationship. Where Jack can lose himself in flights of fancy, Henry was certain to remit the rent on time. Jack might forget what day of the week it is. Henry, never. The hydro, the telephone, the credit card payment, never a day late.

Engrossed in the book he's reading, the article he's writing, his research, Jack will sometimes forget to eat. It was always Henry who snapped him back into the real world and tantalized him with a delicious meal concocted from, sometimes, scant ingredients.

Jack wonders, *how could I have let it all slip away...?*

Thinking about the late hour, he almost turns back. He wonders if it might be better to call in the middle of the day when there's more traffic on The Administration's vast calls database, when there's so much more to check at any second. It could make it more difficult to weed out his call from amongst all others; easier for the system to lose him.

There's no point in that. He knows even now that a camera somewhere has sensed his presence; is recording a man in a hoodie making a call on a dark street from a phone booth with a scratched-out face recognition lens. Even wearing a hoodie might prove futile. When he turns from the phone, a camera placed somewhere, at an exact position, might still pick up his angular features. Then again, the hoodie creates obscuring shadows to combine with the moonless night. Each action, even small ones, makes him feel like his public profile is shrinking. Over time and with luck, he might disappear altogether.

He picks up the receiver and dials.

To his surprise, the other end picks up after only two rings. The sound of the answerer fumbling with the phone. Henry, shocked out of baffling dreams, his voice dry and raspy from sleeping with a gaping mouth as usual.

"Hello...?"

"It's me."

"Jack...!"

Jack winces.

"Sorry about the late hour."

"You were never good with time."

Long seconds tick past while each one waits for the other to speak; for Jack to explain why he'd felt compelled to respond to Henry's plea; for Henry to explain why he'd made his vital request.

At last, Henry speaks.

"Yelena's Eveningsong is tomorrow...." A second to check the clock. "Well today, I guess."

"Yelena...?"

Outward silence. But inside, bursting with sound, image, and memory. Then Henry again.

"It's been a long time, I know, but..."

"I'd forgotten she was older than us."

Another pause while Jack organizes his thoughts. "What time?"

"Eleven-thirty-two."

"In the a.m.?"

"About the time she was born, I assume. Sixty years to the minute. A nice rounding-off to a life."

"That's Yelena...."

More silence. Remembered moments. Sorrow.

"Please come, Jack."

"There'll be eyes there. I try to avoid them nowadays."

"Yelena meant so much to us." And then, a last appeal. "It's vital I see you...."

There's that word again.

"I'll consider it, Henry."

He winces at his own slip.

He hangs up the phone, conscious that they'd used real names on the call.

Henry,

Yelena,

Jack....

***

Thunder...

The sky splitting...

Deluge...

Gutters overflowing...

Streets like rivers.

Jack crams his umbrella into a trashcan; its ribs, bent beyond tolerance; broken. Its solar skin torn; blown inside out by a sudden gust.

The day, drab and torrential like a funeral scene in a movie. Appropriate for Yelena's Eveningsong. Dramatic. Like she was.

Is....

At least until the infusion.

Jack squeezes under a narrow eave. He stands on tiptoe, back pressed against a brick wall as he struggles to keep his feet dry. Like a stick, arms pressed at his sides to avoid the drips. It'll be over soon, like most storms nowadays. A sudden torrent worthy of Noah. Then the break.

Dissolution...

The clouds evaporating...

Sun returning...
Humidity...
Swelter...
A biblical rainbow.

Minutes later, he hops over a rivulet flowing along the gutter to the overburdened catch basin, bubbling up; recent refurbishments to the sewage system, still unable to manage such onslaughts. He rubs the droplets off his wristwatch. He still might make it on time to The Amphorium.

Built for Eveningsong, The Amphorium is a made-up term for a place that sounds official, but benign. It's like an embrace; a womb; curved walls, domed ceiling, ambient calm. Large enough to seat a couple hundred, if the future-deceased was well-loved and well-lived. Or less. Either way, there's intimacy, peace. Either way, The Administration encourages the populace to attend the rites. Even those who don't know the future-deceased.

A way of dispelling fear of one's own impending Eveningsong.

A steel-blue electric zips by, splashing Jack's cuffs; his shoes now beyond salvage; his socks squish between his toes like a sopping sponge. He hopes that when he arrives at The Amphorium, others, like him now, will smell like wet sheep.

Today's not a day to stand out.

It's Yelena's day.

She: a long-time friend. Soft. Capacious. Huggable. She: a cussing, plain-spoken lesbian, and him only desirous of men. A hug between them is just that and only that, a hug. She of the voluminous breasts worthy of laying a head on when in need of mother-earth-comfort. A raucous laugh to shake dust off the rafters: "*Come here, ya big baby.*" Her voice like a wagging finger. Then, whether four or forty, she pulls you into her warmth and kisses the top of your head. Kisses away all life's booboos.

Now, her end; her dissolution. Moments made memory. Over time, drifting away like origami boats set out on a rolling tide. Soon inundated, they sink to unfathomable depths, no longer contemplated daily, if ever.

Aware of time, Jack hopscotches through a minefield of puddles and picks up his pace. He dodges oncoming pedestrians fixated on their electronic devices, and huffs when he arrives at the corner. The traffic light flashes red. All around him, cell phones ping. The Administration's marketing database informs pedestrians they have neared a shop selling items based on their preferences: authentic dark roast coffee, prom dresses, metal wall art or more obscure items like vintage Chinese checkers.

Fixated on her device, a woman in red shoes, unmindful of the red light, ambles through the crowd waiting at the corner. She steps off the curb into oncoming traffic. If it'd been a driverless car, it would've sensed her presence and stopped. But it isn't.

So, tragedy…

Someone's mother, sister, wife, lover struck down. One of her red shoes lands in the opposite gutter like a blood splatter.

The driver of the car, himself distracted with the pings from his device, looks up only after hearing the thud; sees Raggedy Ann float through the air and wrap herself around the base of a lamppost on the opposite corner.

Well-placed cameras record all the relevant details: identity of the victim, the driver, onlookers, and witnesses. All sent to The Administration's accidents database, which notifies police and ambulance. Also, the news media, which, in an instant, screams out the news to smartphones everywhere; 'ACCIDENT AT 4th & MAIN. BYPASS AREA.'

Ping!

Jack's glad that three years ago he cast his cell phone into the river; drowned it. Not only is he not pestered by notifications every few paces, but he's also less on the radar. Still, there are the cameras, recording details; ready to name faces, or within minutes of an accident, relay an ad for life insurance.

Ping!

Glancing at his wristwatch, he feels callous, fearing he might never make it to Yelena's Eveningsong on time. But an officer materializes out of nowhere and encourages onlookers to move on…

"We have all the details. If we need you, we'll

call…."

Sirens…

Police arrive…

An ambulance.

Nothing for Jack to do but leave. With one last glance at the anonymous corpse—somebody's somebody—covered over in haste with a bright yellow blanket, he turns and walks away at a slower pace.

Today seems to be all about death.

***

The sun re-emerges, approaching noon's arc. It sears.

It glints off the white limestone Amphorium.

Celebrants file in like ants, believing in martyrdom for the sake of all others.

Forcing joy.

Believing it's all for the best.

That if humankind is to survive, there must be sacrifice.

Believing in heaven and God.

Or not.

And if not, believing in giving the earth a fighting chance to breathe again.

Where polar icecaps unshrink, the waters refresh.

Where there are fewer particulates in the air.

Oceans recede and redefined seaboards

remember their history.

With a better balance between heat and ice.

Where species thrive; fulfil their purpose in the scheme of things.

A return to seasons.

Jack arrives, still sopping, and takes it all in. Today is Yelena's day. Today, the world will change. It may be better, or it may be worse. For whom can say Yelena's end will make the world a better place. One day beyond her sixtieth birthday might make all the difference. It may be the day she, and she alone, solves the world's problems; creates something; has the right thought; insight. Discovers.

But no...

A decision made during Reckoning; that keeping the population low is the path to survival. A person's life has always been finite. But now, finite is sixty years: rich or poor, powerful, or low, in good health or ill.

Sixty.

And given that rule, that law, a person must decide. Does one accept finite as defined and drift into oblivion with peaceful infusion and celebration? Or does one choose to go down swinging? Gone-wild limbs forced into restraints, a painful jab of the needle instead of the more peaceful slow drip.

There are those who choose rebellion, even at the last minute.

There are those who try to escape

beforehand, forcing The Administration to use myriad methods to track them down and bring them back. Sometimes, with violence.

Jack wonders which Yelena will opt for, acceptance or rebellion. She has not tried to escape in advance. She's always said she believes in the greater good, in sacrifice. But others said so too until the time came; a good vein found for the infusion; the gateway to the network of all other veins and arteries; gutters throughout the body; conjoining rivulets all flowing toward the catch basin. The heart.

Then eternal sleep.

Jack wonders who he will be in Yelena's story. Acceptor of the rule—the law. Or loved one who throws himself on the celebrant crying out, "No!" Amphorium Associates dragging him away so as not to make the day about him. So as not to disturb the celebrated; make her doubt; so as not to disturb the other celebrants; make them fret about their own eventual end, whether impending or years off. Their own Eveningsong.

All will contemplate death during the rites. But to make them fret…?

Then he sees Henry.

He's in deep discussion with a group of three others; two men and a woman, all in their twenties. Each of the men has a solar knapsack. Like solar umbrellas, they became popular the instant they hit the market. One can charge his electronic devices while carrying them on his back. Like so many electrical things nowadays, they're never without power if there's even modest sunlight. The woman carries another popular item, a bulging carryall with intricate embroidery of flora. They appear fanciful because they no longer exist as far as anyone knows. Remembrance of things past. A future promise to bring it all back. The embroidery threads also hold solar properties.

A group of friends in respectful conversation at a friend's Eveningsong. Not unusual. What is unusual, though, is the way the group dissolves, scatters; each person in a different direction when they see Jack approach. Henry, who looked serious and concerned during the discussion, now turns his face to Jack, projecting a sheepish grin. The grin from long-gone days when caught red-handed planning a surprise birthday party or hiding Christmas gifts. However, there's something different about today's smile. One that might appear when guilty of something slyer.

"Jack, you came…."

He approaches; arms spread wide. This time it's not a respectful handshake after years apart. It's the full-on embrace of a former lover who has never forgotten. Close. Warm. The kind to transfer sweat from skin-to-skin.

There's that erection again.

Jack stands back.

"I thought it right to say goodbye to Yelena. Besides, you said it was vital you see me; talk to me."

"Yes, but not here. Not now."

Glancing at a nearby identity camera; he is more aware than others might be, because nowadays most people have grown to accept them; forgotten they exist.

"Let's go in…."

***

Buffered from outside noise…

Silent, but for the ambient music. New Age, shapeless, yet somehow melodic; it soothes…

The soft murmur of voices…

Curved walls painted soft pink…

Pale grey carpet…

Dim sunlight through a stained-glass dome depicting colourful flora, long since extinct. But something to inspire remembrance of the purpose.

In rows around the room, seats for the celebrants. Each with an unobstructed view of a raised circular platform; the hallowed place of Eveningsong. All seats taken. It'll be a good send-off.

Jack and Henry make their way to the back row and sit. Jack makes out the faces of the three people Henry was speaking to outside. It's curious to him that none of them has sat together. Instead, they sit well apart, as if no thought to reuniting once they'd scattered like chickens fleeing a fox.

Jack turns to Henry.

"Who are your friends?"

"Friends…?"

"The group you were speaking to outside."

"Just people I know."

"I don't believe I've ever met them."

"It's been a while, Jack. There are a lot of people in my life now that you've never met."

Even though Jack instigated the breakup, he aches at the notion that Henry got on with his life, made new friends.

The appointed time nears, and the lights dim…

Walls seem to disappear as projections appear on them…

Trees…

Tall…

Evergreen…

Encircling.

It's as though the assembled have gathered in a glade, deep in a forest. Ferns and other shade plants, existing only in memory for the oldest generation, like Yelena. Plant life that the youngest have never known at all, except in books and at times like this.

Three aisles radiate from the central platform, like paths through the forest. Along two of the paths, a man and a woman appear from the dimness and make their way to the platform. Dressed in flowing white robes and ridiculous artificial laurels, they're like paintings on a Grecian urn. They arrive at the platform and, in silence, step up. Then, from the centre of the stage, a low bed rises, an altar. Covered in crisp white linen, it glows in the dim light now filtering through the stained-glass dome. A glint of sun bounces off a metal stand from which a plastic bag full of infusion dangles, its thin hose trailing like a venomous snake.

Yelena, guided by two Associates, each dressed in flowing robes and false laurels, makes her way along the third aisle. She, dressed in her favourite pinstripe pantsuit, looks serene, accepting. She arrives at the low bed, where she sits and looks out over the assembled. A benign smile. Somehow, she looks more beautiful than Jack or Henry can ever remember. Was she sedated ahead of time, or is this Yelena now? All defiance has left her body, her mind. She takes in a weeping woman sitting in the front row. It looks like the woman might throw herself at Yelena's feet and cry out. But Yelena gives her a sharp look, and the woman recedes into herself.

Today is Yelena's day. There will be no hysteria.

She scans the crowd, picking out faces in the dimness. Her eyes land on Jack and Henry. Her benevolent look says, *"Do not fret over me."*

Then she focuses her gaze upon Henry only. She nods. To Jack, watching on, the nod seems somehow significant, a tacit agreement. A signal.

One of the White-Robes steps forward.

"Does anyone wish to speak? Have stories…?"

Yelena raises her hand.

"There'll be no stories today. You've told me I leave this place a fine woman. You've said I have a kind soul; that I was generous. That I was loving, even when I was demanding."

Her hand drops into her lap.

"I know all this. You all know it. No one need tell me again."

She has not considered that others need to tell their stories. But not now. If she hears them, it may lead her to doubt; to miss her life before it ends. No. Share the stories at the celebration afterwards.

She lays back onto the bed, exposing her arm; a stent inserted beforehand in the found vein; the gutter. One of the Associates moves to her side and inserts the hose. The volume of the ambient music increases, covering the sound of sobs as the infusion wends its way through Yelena's body.

But running beneath it, a heartbeat.

Yelena's.

First strong, then slowing…

Unaware he's doing it; Henry reaches over and takes Jack's hand…

The heartbeat. Slower still…

Jack's mind returns to days gone by. It had always been Henry who had reached out first.

Slowing, slowing…

Jack pushes back his tears.

Slowing, slowing, slowing…

Stopped.

Within minutes, gone.

Henry looks at his wristwatch. 11:33 a.m. One minute away from the promise. Still, it would please Yelena.

After a momentary pause, the bed sinks beneath the platform…

Yelena, vanishing.

Soon the smell of cremation. Her ashes for scattering at her request over a field of wildflowers. If loved ones can find one.

The ambient music, now only an echo. Lights rise, and the projected forest disappears. The actual world returns. Celebrants file out as they had filed in.

The two young men and the woman Henry had spoken to outside are the last to leave.

***

Pastry…
Herbal tea…
Sandwiches…
Stories…
A final release of emotion…
Laughter…
Peace.

Jack looks across the room towards the buffet table, a slight smile appearing as he watches Henry hunched over the pastry tray, struggling to choose from the vast assortment. He's always a sucker for sweets.

After filing out of The Amphorium, the celebrants had gathered at an adjacent building to praise Yelena. Each who was a friend had stories of how they first met her; about how her early struggles for women's rights, which seem to ebb and flow with each changing regime, had inspired them; about how her boundless love had made them feel inadequate in her presence; how her temper could frighten. But a temper never misplaced. If Yelena showed anger, it's because you were wrong and just didn't know it yet. Her forgiveness. A never-hold-a-grudge attitude. Her raucous laugh. Nothing bad remembered or spoken of. Only the good.

Those who didn't know her, or who just came for the sandwiches, listen with respect, and sip their tea.

Henry swallows his third tiny pastry. He turns and sees Jack, alone in a corner, grinning at him. He makes his way across the room. It's time they speak.

"Let's walk."

Jack sets down his teacup and they step through a door to the outside. They amble into a small park across the street. People prize such green spaces nowadays. Still, there aren't too many other amblers. The shade feels cool. Soothing on the skin. Henry, deep in thought, chooses his words with care, assessing whether to trust.

"I don't intend to die, Jack."

"Ever…?"

Henry chuckles.

"I mean, I choose to die from natural causes.

I'll defy Eveningsong."

Jack knows the gravity of that statement. It makes Henry part of the rebellion. It endangers not only him, but those he knows and loves. The Administration goes to any length to enforce conformity, to make an example of the defiant.

Always.

"Listen to me, Jack. I know you agree. When I saw you the other day and you mentioned you don't have a phone, I knew then you're trying to disappear, too."

"I…"

"Your plan may not be my plan, but you have one, I'm certain of it."

Jack looks back at Henry, considering whether asking the next question and hearing an answer might endanger him.

"What's your plan?"

"I trust you, Jack."

Jack nods, aware of identity cameras everywhere.

"I don't know why we broke apart…."

"Oh, but you do, Henry."

A great sadness permeates Henry's pale blue eyes.

"William…."

He takes Jack's hands in his.

"I never blamed you, Jack. You know that. Or you should."

He's desperate to hold Jack. Comfort him. Assure him there's no blame. Instead…

"Come with me, Jack."

"Come…?"

"To The Haven."

Jack blinks.

"The Haven! That's a myth. Something people latch onto when they've lost all hope."

"Oh, it's real."

"It's a trap set by The Administration. They capture anyone who sets out to find it and they bring them back at once."

"The Administration themselves started that rumour, to keep people from even trying. But The Haven's real, Jack."

"Where is it?"

"I can't tell you. Not yet."

Jack stares back at him, unsure what to believe. It's true, he's doing everything he can to disappear, but his plan has more to do with disappearing in plain sight. Not setting out for a fictional dream place.

"We leave at midnight, Jack."

"We…?"

"If you want to meet, call me before eleven from your phone booth and I'll tell you where to meet. After that, I'll be unreachable. My cell phone will be at the bottom of the river."

When he hears that, Jack smiles.

"I love you, Jack. I always will. I want you back in my life. I miss you more than I can bear. But only you can decide. Just remember what The Administration's willing to do with the loved ones of the rebellious."

"But I know nothing."

"They won't stop until they're sure of that themselves."

Each man stands in silence, taking in the rare twitter of a bird. How had things come to this? How had things turned upside down, inside out? Where A is Z and Z is A.

"It'll get rough around here, Jack. Shit's gonna happen."

Jack doesn't want to think about what that means.

"Are you sure you have the strength to flee? You're almost sixty."

Henry laughs.

"You've swallowed the Kool-Ade, kid."

By God, Jack misses him too. Henry's always willing to call bullshit. It's what Jack loves about him.

Henry leans in. "You've already chosen life, Jack. Why else would you be trying to disappear before Eveningsong? Please... consider it."

He turns to leave.

"Eleven, Jack. If it's your choice to come with us, call by eleven."

With this, he's gone.

***

4:00 a.m.
Pre-dawn skies. Purple...
A thin line along the perimeter of the

horizon. Pinkish red…

Birds in the park converse. They herald a new day…

Otherwise, the city, quiet. Unwilling to stir just yet.

It's at least two hours before raised blinds. Windows opened in hopes of air that's not acrid.

Two hours before the first to rise and stray into the streets; streets that border The Amphorium. Even now, in the dark, its white limestone glows, announcing its purpose. An ordinary day that promises to be a busy one, with at least three Eveningsongs planned. But today's not an ordinary day. Today is extraordinary.

From inside The Amphorium, a massive explosion…

Copperplate doors blow out, clear across the street to the park…

The stained-glass dome shatters into a trillion splinters…

Flames, like a volcano, shoot into the night sky…

The city shakes…

Startled birds flee from limbs and ledges…

Alarm bells sound.

Within minutes, sirens. First, a long way off, then nearer, nearer. Louder, louder.

Neighbours rush into the street; stunned, their mouths agape.

Fire trucks arrive, but too late. Flames engulf the building. Walls crumble. The entire dome structure falls.

More vital is to ensure the park across the street doesn't catch fire. They must save it at all costs. People in their nightclothes run through the trees, tamping out stray cinders floating between branches to the ground.

"Thank God there was rain earlier," they say.

Hours later, only rubble…

Broken limestone…

Blackened…

No longer glowing in the morning sun.

CHAPTER 2

A stark blue sky...
Cloudless...
Dehydrating sun...
Intense...
White.

Undulating beneath it, the vast Atlantic. Vaster now than in recent history.

The ocean, swirling through the remains of a mega-city, once bustling. Deserted high-rises now jut from the sea, resembling inundated tombstones.

Waves crashing onto a beach that was once distant suburbia. Now, dotted here and there with the ruins of wood-framed houses, long since abandoned; weather-beaten; crumbling into the sand.

Beyond that, dunes, swallowing up farmland.

Bounding over the mounds, an electric dune buggy; the driver, fearless. Wind coursing through thick brown hair and beating against the ruddy skin of a handsome face. Teeth clenched. Goggled eyes intense. The eyes of a man with a mission, for indeed, there must be one.

Arriving at the edge of the beach, the driver cranks the wheel, skidding sideways, sending up a wall of sand and screeching to a halt. After spitting out a mouthful of grit, Administration Officer Alistair Goodwin steps out of the buggy and wanders to the water's edge. Taking out binoculars, he scans the distant tombstones.

It had happened fast; seaboard towns and cities swamped as if overnight; island-nations consumed; the entire state of Florida, gone. Hundreds of thousands had no time to flee. Hundreds of thousands more, displaced. The earth had enough. Roaring. Retaking control. No matter humankind, the planet is determined to survive, in one form or another. An ecosystem altered; unrecognizable to what came before. And unless fitted into the new ecology on nature's terms, humankind will perish.

Peering through the binoculars, Alistair Goodwin can still make out his family tombstone. Living on one of the lower floors, his young wife and son had no chance of escaping when the tidal wave came, swept them away, while Alistair was in the middle of the country on business. Even though it was hopeless, and a desperate man could not have saved his loved ones, to this day, Alistair dreams of being there during the flood; of dying together. Now, to live is to ache. To experience endless, roiling anger; a man who had survived Reckoning.

Anarchic...

Bloody...

Lawless.

After the inundation, the first instinct was nationalist and insular. Marauders took over cities and towns, scrambling to define territory, pillaging. Until finally, an international body of like-minded Youngers formed and took control. Gone was the politicising old guard, who were well beyond finite as defined.

A new regime, The Administration, arose with one goal: survival of humankind against a newly hostile planet. Controlled territories meant nothing. Borders meant nothing. Defined countries meant nothing. For the first time in known history, "Each-one-for-Everyone" became the law. Using technology; eyes everywhere, The Administration squelched rebellion, and abolished prisons now considered unnecessary. Anyone who refuses to follow the laws of Each-One-For-Everyone and Eveningsong, "disappears." There's no conscience. Population reduction is the end goal. Stopping the domino effect of climate change is paramount. Alistair agreed and, at first chance, left his job as a geologist with an oil company and joined The Administration to hunt and disappear anyone who tries to escape Eveningsong, the law of finite.

Squinting one last time through the

binoculars, Alistair makes the usual promise: to return on this date, a year from now, the anniversary of the inundation. And each year until October twelfth, twenty-five years from now, his sixtieth birthday, his Eveningsong. If Eveningsong is still the law by then. If humankind survives the new planet, the new ecology. Then he can join his young wife and son in a great beyond in which he never used to believe.

    But now, he must.
    There lies hope…
    The end of anger…
    The end of his ache.

***

    A bed-sitting room…
    Scrubbed and polished to a high gleam…
    Orderly.
    A family photograph on the desk: Alistair, Melinda, young Nicholas; the one Alistair used to carry in a suitcase during business travel. Now, the photograph is the only thing left from a former life.
    On the wall above the desk, a perfectly aligned grid of framed butterflies; colourful, exotic, rare. A collection only found at estate sales nowadays. Authentication required that the collection existed long before the inundation. Today, the law forbids the capture of butterflies for one's own use. The rules protect such diminishing species, hoping they still exist in small numbers in

far corners of the world.

Poaching is now punishable by death.

Alistair runs a hand over a framed monarch butterfly. Once abundant, yet thinning long before the change; a warning sign to those in charge who were more focused on the interests of whomever contributed big money to personal political campaigns. Usually, captains of the fossil fuel industry, of which Alistair was a part. Political survival was paramount. The monarch butterflies be damned. Alistair flinches at the memory of young Nicholas coming home from elementary school and lambasting oil interests. *"You're killing the planet, Daddy."* Alistair hugged and kissed Nicholas and reminded him that oil money bought him the LEGOS he loved so much.

The Legos themselves, a by-product of oil.

Legos, which, tragically, washed away with him.

In memory of Nicholas, Alistair had bought the butterfly collection from the widow of a professor of entomology at a small mid-western university, shedding her possessions to prepare for her Eveningsong.

Alistair bumps up a laptop, then clicks on a file labelled 'Amphorium.' The blowing up of the sacred building was a shock. And unless The Administration does something, tracks those responsible and holds them accountable, others may follow the example. Nothing must weaken faith in The Administration.

Within minutes of the incident, The Administration began compiling information from its various databases, fact-based files, and cameras in the streets around The Amphorium in the days leading up to the blast. Faces matched to those suspected of belonging to the rebellion. There were possibilities. The Administration had named and tracked most suspects, except five who vanished from the city.

Alistair clicks on a video file, focusing on a small group gathered for the recent Eveningsong of one Yelena Chomsky, former librarian. There are three men and a woman. One man has grown long hair and a beard. Men do this to confuse the identity cameras.

It doesn't work.

Both men carry solar knapsacks and the woman, one of those popular embroidered carryalls. None carry these articles back out when exiting The Amphorium after Yelena's Eveningsong. The third man: tall, slender, silver hair; one, Henry Chagall. Another librarian at the same library as Yelena Chomsky. A camera in the park across the street from The Amphorium had later recorded Henry walking there with Jack Parnell, his husband. Parnell was a onetime journalist who is clearly trying to disappear. His profile shows less information over the past few years. The facts show that Jack Parnell and Henry Chagall are legally married and had adopted an infant son; one William Chagall-Parnell. An impoverished drug-addicted mother rejected him at birth upon learning of his Downes Syndrome. Jack and Henry raised the child lovingly into young adulthood. Then, because of Reckoning, and because of his mental deficiency, William's Eveningsong was early and abrupt.

That last fact jolts Alistair. Clicking out of the file, he shuts the laptop.

But not before the entire video file mysteriously becomes pixilated and disappears.

***

Arborite. White with gold flecks…

Glistening chrome…

Banquettes padded with red vinyl…

Black and white ceramic tile. Gleaming. Reflective…

A frosted sign etched into a plate-glass window: 'The Un-Greasy Spoon.'

Hanging on the walls, photographs of old-time movie stars from long-gone-days.

The first time Alistair walked through the door; he instantly took to the place. It was a throwback to an era he had never occupied, but one that engendered comfort. Besides which, underneath the smell of toasted club sandwiches, french-fries, and faux coffee, the place smelled clean.

To complete the vintage vibe, the servers wear retro uniforms and sport tags with fake names such as Midge, Zeek and Veronica. The menu is a throwback too, except none of the meat is real and the coffee is fake.

Alistair slides into his usual booth. Today's server is Bette. No doubt so named for her Bette Davis eyes.

"The usual Tuesday breakfast…?"

"Please."

(Fake steak, two eggs sunny-up, home fries, two slices of tomato, toast with jam, faux coffee with milk-and-sugar).

He's flattered, she remembers. Then again, he comes here routinely, ordering the same Monday breakfast (oatmeal), Tuesday (steak and eggs), Wednesday (French toast), etcetera. It never varies.

Alistair used to wonder if Bette's flirty smile was true, or charm-for-tips. Over and over, he's asked her real name. She never takes the bait or breaks out of her role, so it's the latter. He often wonders if she'd let him bed her. It's been a while. Still, best to keep it business only, even if Bette finds him charming. Besides, if he fucked her and things got weird, he'd have to search for a new diner. Today he's more hungry than horny. Given a choice between Bette and breakfast, he chooses breakfast.

Bette fills a mug with steaming coffee. They call it coffee, but just like the *faconbacon*, it isn't real. Shipping the real stuff halfway around the world, nowadays, uses too many resources, making the price of a cup astronomical. So instead, chicory root or roasted ground up acorns. And, for the same reason, no more delicious Assam tea. Only what's at hand: chamomile, peppermint, or lemongrass. Like the fake meat, it isn't horrible. But Alistair longs for black tea with its tannins, and real coffee with its caffeine kick.

With the threat hanging over the grain and seed crops which feed the chickens, even eggs may be hard to come by soon. And bread for the toast. Alistair doesn't want to think about it. Not today. Instead, he'll savour every bite and sip and be grateful.

He bumps up his tablet and scans the news. The Administration is still pumping out stories detailing the bombing of The Amphorium, each the same story. There's no questioning the motives of someone who'd do such a thing: *an enemy of the people; a threat to order, peace, and harmony; a breaker of the law of Each-one-for-Everyone.* Of course, it's futile for him/her/they to believe in escaping justice. The Administration's big data will sweep them up in no time.

Anyway, that's what the stories say.

Bette Davis flashes a gleaming smile as she sets out the full meal Alistair ordered.

"Anything else, hon?"

Alistair plays the game.

"Thanks, doll. Ketchup?"

Bette gives a wink, happy to accept an in-character flirt. From an adjacent booth, she retrieves a bottle of ketchup. When she sets it on

Alistair's table, she leans over just enough to show cleavage. Alistair would consider it beyond sexist if Zeek hadn't joined in too and padded his crotch. Eye candy for the ladies. And a man or two. If he isn't padding, good on him. Everybody needs to figure a way to squeeze out an extra buck or two in tips.

Alistair bites into his veggie-based steak. It isn't horrible. Still, there's something in the texture that isn't right. The lack of enough real fat. The lack of blood.

As he chews through his meal, he scans more bombing stories, stopping at a picture of the smoking rubble. He knows what he must do when he catches the perpetrators.

Still, he mustn't let that thought ruin breakfast.

He swallows the last of the chicory brew, then raises his empty cup to Bette, signalling a refill. As he does so, he glimpses a man watching him from across the room. Mid-fifties, or almost sixty. It's difficult to be certain. The man looks away, but not before Alistair takes in "that thing." It's taken him a while to figure out. But he now knows "that thing" relates to the uniform.

He felt proud when he first took The Beige.

Trim. Neat. Inoffensive colour.

Authoritative with its smart, creaseless worsted fabric.

A uniform that, at first, put people at ease. Signalled order in the streets. Laws upheld. Safety.

Instead, what he now sees in the man's eyes; indeed, in the eyes of the majority lately, is something he dislikes.

Anxiety…

Even fear of him.

***

An expansive warehouse building…

Overhead lights dimmed…

The air kept purposely chilly…

A maze of cubicles…

Endless.

Each booth is part of a colour-coded grouping. From green for finance, to red for politics. And all imaginable colours and traits.

Each cubicle housing a computer with a glowing screen.

Hunched over each keyboard and clicking mouse, an Administration Researcher. Each dressed in a jacket matching their colour-coded booth. Each investigating only a part of a picture; a part of a person. Only Senior Administrators housed on an upper level ringing the hall allowed to draw the pieces together into a cohesive profile when necessary.

At least that's the theory.

Alistair ambles through the maze, past booth after booth after colour-coded booth. The soft clicking on keyboards; the slide of the mouse across the pad. Otherwise, silence.

Focus.

Arriving at a corkscrew stair, he climbs to the balcony level overlooking the entire room. Gazing out over the rail at the colour-coded maze below, he thinks of a giant Rubik's Cube. Each side twisted and twirled until it resolves into a single-coloured patch: yellow, blue, white. Each patch in this place, serving a prescribed role.

He steps into the glass-walled office of The Senior and addresses a man standing in front of an entire wall of video monitors.

"Senior...."

Alistair has always found the term amusing because the man he addresses as Senior is at least five years younger than him.

The man turns.

Handsome. Square-jawed. Insecure beneath his stern look.

"Goodwin. I've been waiting."

He likes to make it known to everyone that he's always waiting. Even when the person he meets arrives on time or even early. He motions towards one screen and the image of another man, younger than Alistair, piped in remotely from his administrative vehicle. "You know Bateman...."

"Yes, sir." He raises his hand at the screen.

Bateman returns a perfunctory wave.

"He'll be collaborating with you on this one."

Alistair dislikes Bateman. He'd started out all right. But, over time, he's become arrogant, smug. An officer who provokes fear of the uniform. The fear that Alistair sensed in the eyes of the old man at the diner. He and Bateman joined The Administration around the same time and trained together at The Academy.

Reserved at first, even shy, Bateman grew up on a farm in the middle of the country. Then he took The Beige. Instead of dignified authority, he imbues the uniform with coerciveness. He grew a Van Dyke to hide his weak chin and rarely removes his dark glasses, even indoors as though he wants to hide his inability to look people straight in the eye. And although he's tall, he adds an extra quarter inch to the soles of his shoes and another quarter inch with inside lifts. He's developed a cocky strut with his thumbs always in his belt. When he approaches the citizenry, he stands too close, with his legs spread and his chest puffed out.

Confrontational…

Calculated intimidation.

Alistair dislikes it.

The Senior flicks a switch on his desk, and the glass walls of his office become opaque.

Instant privacy.

Then he clicks a remote. Images of five people appear on various screens: two men and a woman, all in their mid-twenties. There are also two men in their late-fifties and nearing the age of Eveningsong. Alistair recognizes each of them from the profiles he studied.

"The data leads us to believe that these five people carried out the bombing and they're travelling together."

Without warning, and just as happened on Alistair's laptop, the images of the five faces pixilate and vanish from the screens. Perplexed, The Senior clicks the remote repeatedly.

Nothing.

"Hmm...."

He keys in data on his keyboard, bringing up traffic-cam images of various freeways and roads running in and out of the city. He clicks the remote again, freezing an image.

"We believe they're travelling together in this RV."

Alistair squints at the fuzzy image of a large RV; white with a thin blue stripe running along its sides, front to back. The timestamp on the image reads 12:26 a.m.

The Senior unfreezes the image.

Bateman speaks up. "It makes sense they'd get the hell outta Dodge hours before the bombing."

Alistair smirks at the macho phrase, "get the hell outta Dodge." He leans in, squinting at the moving image.

"But how can you know it's them? The shadows are dense. You can't make out who's driving."

"It fits their profiles, and..."

Bateman interrupts.

"The data's never wrong."

The Senior clicks the remote again, calling up live drone footage of the RV from above, now travelling along a country road.

"They evaded us briefly. But then a drone caught them exiting a travel park early this morning."

"Do you know where they're headed?"

Bateman again, "Where they always do...."

***

Bateman snaps shut his laptop, cutting off the conference call with The Senior and Goodwin. He climbs out of his vehicle.

Another stark blue sky...

Another intense sun...

The kind that sears unprotected skin without sunscreen, SPF 50.

A narrow ribbon of highway stretching through vast cornfields...

The vociferous chirping of cicadas in an otherwise still afternoon...

Administration vehicles lined up along the road's gravel shoulders...

Two dozen of The Beige, leaning. Waiting. Weapons at the ready...

A barricade stretched across the road, although no traffic. Sometimes a lone farmer driving a sputtering tractor.

Bateman sniffs the air.

Smoke from a major bush fire, somewhere, miles away. A lightning strike on dry tinder caused it. Now out of control, it has burned for days. It has yet to reach the cornfields. It must never.

Firefighters must corral it no matter the costs.

But the fire is not Bateman's worry. His task, one thing, and one thing only; pull over the RV passing through his sector, capture the alleged perpetrators, and hold them until Alistair Goodwin arrives to interrogate them, and then return them to the city for trial.

He drags a long stray black hair from his sleeve. From where did that come? He glances at Administration Officer Lila Wong, her bluish-black hair drawn together into a tight chignon. Had she been so close that a stray hair could land on him? Yes. He remembers now. She had brushed past him as they piled into their vehicles to come to this site.

He evokes her smell…

Fresh…

Meant to conjure a sea breeze.

"They should be here soon…."

Bateman snaps back into the present moment. "Huh…?"

Lila looks towards him with a tight smile, sensing she's brought him back from one of his macho fantasies.

Bateman forces nonchalance.

"Not long now."

It's a matter of course. A thing he supervises each day.

The world has settled after Reckoning. More or less. Still, there are pockets of resistance. But the alleged perpetrators in the RV, seeing two dozen armed Beige, will no doubt surrender. They always do. The event will unfold without incident, the same as all other failed rebellion.

Truth-be-told, Bateman loves times such as these. He pictures himself, as always, barking out orders at the perpetrators to exit the vehicle with hands raised, then to lie on the pavement, now buckling in the heat. Officers cuffing hands behind backs.

Of course—and this makes his heart race faster—there's another scenario. With nothing to lose, the perps might opt to crash through the roadblock; make a run for it. A ludicrous chase with a dozen police vehicles careening through cornfields in pursuit of a ridiculously large RV, its hubcaps flying. A final shootout—for indeed, they must have an arsenal. The perpetrators, dead in one final blaze of glory. Only a flesh wound for him…

A medal of honour.

"I think I see it…."

Lila again.

Wiping sweat from his brow, Bateman squints through the wavy heat. There, approaching from afar, the white RV glistening in the sun. Hovering over it, a small dot. A drone with a cam, relaying the action live to Administration Headquarters; footage from the drone and from body cams fed into the massive databases for broadcast live across all platforms.

Bateman smooths his hair and straightens

his uniform as he moves to the centre of the road in front of the barricade. Standing feet apart, he waves his arms casually, flagging the RV. At once, it slows and comes to a halt, almost touching his puffed-out chest.

There will be no chase today.

Disappointed, Bateman gives a quick glance at the drone hovering overhead, then barks out the usual commands.

"Exit the vehicle, now. Hands in the air!"

Rifles snap to shoulders as the door to the RV slides open.

A man and a woman, mid-thirties, step out; hands raised; wide-eyed; trembling, followed by three terrified, sobbing children.

Behind his dark glasses, Bateman scrunches his eyes.

Back at Administration Headquarters, Alistair, viewing the live drone feed, notices there is no thin blue line painted along the sides of the RV.

CHAPTER 3

Jack…

Gazing up at millions of stars…

Millions…!

Freckling a plum-coloured sky.

Silence. Except for the sound of Henry's soft snore, asleep beside him; their seats in a MINI Cooper fully reclined. Two tall men stretched out as much as they can be in a cramped car.

Jack, looking up through a skylight…

Millions of stars…

Thinking how long it's been since he's lain next to Henry, sleeping; wanting to slide his hand into his; to know again that in his sleep, Henry's limp fingers will instinctively come alive and entwine in his.

But no. He mustn't.

It's come to this. Five people fleeing the city together in a nondescript van hours before the timed explosion. Arriving in a small sleeping town in the middle of the night. Each transferring to separate vehicles left there beforehand and then heading off in separate directions. All prearranged well in advance. And in case The Administration captures any member of the team, each person's destination unknown to the others. Only Jack and Henry travelling together. Jack, who has nothing to do with a bomb plot. Caught in fate, compelling him to make the call to Henry; to go along with his plan; to meet up at midnight and escape the city with him.

Now, here…

In a farmer's field…

In darkness…

Looking up through a skylight at stars in a purple sky.

Can he slip out of the car without waking Henry?

He pulls the latch and pushes open the door. Henry stirs, suddenly alert.

"Shh…. We're safe. I just need to piss."

Henry settles back into guarded sleep.

Jack shuts the door to keep the bugs out; bugs that sense a target and at once go on the attack. Even Jack's penis as he pisses on the grass. But bugs are a good thing, aren't they? A signal of recovery. He brushes away a blood sucking mosquito and zips up, then pulls up the hood on his jacket. He wants to run. Not from bugs. Nor from Henry, asleep in a MINI Cooper. Not from rebels or bombs…

From William.

His spirit, ever present, often keeps Jack

awake. But he's especially forceful tonight.

It must be the stars.

Millions....

Jack conjures a memory of him and William, twelve years old at the time, sitting for hours, cutting out cardboard stars with safety scissors. William's full concentration, tongue sticking out of the side of his mouth. Then covering the stars with tinfoil and hanging them from threads above William's bed. In the soft glow of a nightlight, they dazzled. Night after night, Jack watched him; his almond-shaped eyes taking in the sparkle until slipping into peaceful sleep.

Loving...

Harmless...

Innocent...

Smiling...

Not a mean thought.

Jack flinches at the memory.

How could he have let them take him? How could he not free himself from their grip? To fight until death.

He wants to run through the field and never stop. To outrun the purple sky; outrun the stars until he drops; to never revive again. He wants to run from William's horrified cries.

"Dadda...! Dadda...!"

To run from the memory of a child's mind in a young man's body; from William's outstretched hands, grasping as they dragged him away.

"Dadda...! Dadda...!"

But he can't outrun the sky.

And there will always be stars.

He walks towards a lone tree in the middle of the field and sits on a large rock beneath it. The field slopes to a distant road. Is that the road they'll travel together? To escape? Henry spoke of The Haven. Does it exist? Is it somewhere at the end of that road? No room for those thoughts just now. William is too strong, haunting, occupying too much space. If he sits there on the rock under the tree, waiting for the sun to rise, watching the stars fade, William will fade too.

No…

William never fades.

Are the others from the group in similar fields near a similar road? Their way to freedom. Beyond their names, Jack knows nothing. Henry refuses even to divulge his own role in the plot. Jack is uncertain that he's even given real names: Sasha, Yeorgi, Elizabeth. Each mid-to-late-twenties. Each with a grudge against The Administration to be sure, and for their own reasons determined to destroy it.

On the one hand, he wishes he knew more.

On the other, the possibility of capture is real.

The less known, the better.

***

Elizabeth, alone…

Leaning against her silver-coloured electric,

at the edge of an expansive wind farm...

Turbines dotted everywhere, stretching as far as the distant horizon...

Lofty...

Elegant...

Painted white. Set against a deep blue sky in an emerald pasture where black and white cattle used to graze.

Blades spinning in a thin breeze, contributing power to augment the nuclear grid. Something The Administration got right.

In the middle of it, and out of place, a decrepit house. It used to belong to a family of ranchers, stretching back generations. Elizabeth's family. The house abandoned after the cattle industry collapsed and The Administration expropriated the land for the massive wind farm. The house left standing instead of flattened. Engulfed. Flecks of white paint now peeling off its clapboard siding, turning grey. Left to rot on its own.

Elizabeth, now standing in what used to be a cozy living room.

Layer upon layer of wallpaper dating back to great grandmother, peeling, water stained. Blue squares overlaying yellow polka dot overlaying beige stripes overlaying bouquets of dusty-pink Victorian roses.

Windowpanes shattered...

Moth-eaten curtain ruffling in the breeze...

Floorboards buckling...

Plaster falling...
Lath exposed...
Sparrow's nest in an upper corner...
Cobwebs...
The smell of dust...

Ancient soot from the crumbling fireplace, sent adrift by a draft sucked through cracks in the bricks.

Elizabeth, now standing in the kitchen.

Cupboard doors hanging from rusted hinges...

An old gas-stove...

The fridge, its door ripped away...

A battered table...

Broken chairs...

Shattered beer bottles in the corners. Remnants of invading teenage partiers.

Elizabeth, climbing the stair. Stepping into what used to be her bedroom. And generations of daughters before her.

Floor creaking...

The old iron bedstead she used to hate...

"Please, mom and dad. It sags. Can't we get a new bed?"

Someone has dragged the old, musty mattress to the floor.

Discarded condoms nearby...

Evidence of illicit teenage rutting.

Elizabeth, walking back across the field towards her car.

Being here is dangerous. Surely The

Administration knows this place. It's part of her history, her profile, if they can decrypt it. Having once worked for them, she knows profiles. Now part of the rebellion, she must never return, seek reflection. Only move forward to an uncertain future…

To escape.

Elizabeth, driving away in her silver-coloured electric. Not looking back…

Merging onto the busy superhighway running alongside the wind farm…

Every second vehicle painted the same silver colour as Elizabeth's. Indistinguishable, one from the other…

Anonymous…

Elizabeth, disappearing.

***

Oppressive heat…

Humidity. Even at midnight…

Sweat drips from Yeorgi's newly shaved head and into his eyes…

His T-shirt sticks to his chest and back…

He raises his arms, sniffing his pits…

"Jesus…."

It's a risk being here; in a dark corner across the street from Katarina's flat. But he wants to see her.

More truthfully, he wants to see Trinket. Just one last time.

A half hour ago he parked his pickup in an

alley, blocks away and made his way here, always crossing to the other side of the street whenever anyone neared him. Now, he looks up at an open second-floor window; at Katarina's shadow passing back and forth in the light behind a shabby window shade.

Things had ended with a nasty divorce. Katarina was greedy about the kid. She went for full custody and got it. The "esteemed" judge believed Katarina's description of Yeorgi's overheated temper. And disbelieved Yeorgi when he told her that Katarina, and everyone else in the world, just misunderstands him. It didn't help that he was confrontational throughout court proceedings. The Judge granted him controlled access only.

Now, as a man escaping, he can no longer go once a week for supervised visits with the kid.

So, here…

On a dim street in the humidity at midnight…

Imperilling himself.

He surveys the street to make sure that, in a dark corner, no one lays in wait to seize him when he knocks at his ex-wife's door. But he's willing to chance it to see Trinket for one last time.

Katarina always accuses him of being a terrible father, even though he's never missed a support payment. Not one. It's not for Katarina's sake that he does it, but for Trinket. It's not the child's fault that her parents can't cooperate; that they know how to push each other's buttons; that, without fail, things degrade into a power struggle. His love for Trinket overwhelms him and he can't bear the notion that he'll never see her again. But that's the scenario. If he vanishes completely, he'll never see her. If The Administration catches him, he's a dead man. Either way, Trinket will grow up without a father. As he had.

Standing there in the midnight heat, Yeorgi wonders how things could have spiralled so out of control.

His passions have always led him, whether in politics or in his love life. In Katarina's case, his penis led the way. He'd picked her up in a bar: she, wearing the tightest of dresses that accentuated her curves and ample breasts. Sexually charged, his handsome Slavic face enamoured her, even though she initially had her eye on an older, more prosperous looking man at the other end of the bar.

She and Yeorgi enjoyed a heated first encounter, with sex verging on violence; destroying the bedroom furniture. Their thrashing shattered a bedside lamp. So it was, for the first months of their relationship, until Katarina became pregnant. After that, things cooled. Still wanting to party, Katarina contemplated aborting the fetus, but Yeorgi convinced her to keep the child. And even though his gut counselled otherwise, he proposed marriage. And even though Katarina's gut screeched, she accepted. From then on, things worsened. In the end, Yeorgi's explosive temper and Katarina's tendency to carp turned to violence on both sides, leading to blackened eyes, busted lips, and broken hearts; locked doors kicked in and shattered dishes until each had enough. Yeorgi walked out, vowing to fight for his rights to the kid and with Katarina vowing to destroy him using any means possible.

Now here...

In darkness...

In the stifling heat...

Running from an administration determined to execute him.

With one last scan of the street, he steps out of the shadows and crosses to a door leading to Katarina's flat. He presses a button on the intercom and waits.

Finally, a wary voice. "Hello...?"

"Katarina...? It's me."

Shocked silence, then, "Yeorgi, what the hell...?"

"Let me in Kat."

"What are you doing here?"

"Kat, please. It's dangerous out here."

After interminable silence, a buzzer sounds and the lock on the door releases. Yeorgi slips inside and climbs the steep, narrow stair.

A door opens on the second floor, and Katarina pokes her head out. Panicky, she looks up the hall at other doors leading to neighbouring flats. Fearful, she jerks her head at Yeorgi, and he rushes into her rooms.

"The Beige have been all over me. If anybody sees you…"

"I won't stay long."

He looks around, taking in the scruffy room.

Cigarette butts overflowing an ashtray…

A half-glass of whiskey…

The television tuned to a late-night movie…

A sink full of dirty dishes in the kitchenette…

Soiled clothes strewn here and there…

A child's toys.

"Still not the best housekeeper, I see."

"Really…? You came here to fight?"

Yeorgi realizes he's overstepped a boundary; something he vowed not to do this time. He pulls back.

Katarina takes him in icily as she pulls her silk robe over an exposed nipple.

"You shaved your head. And your beard." She huffs, "Not much of a disguise."

Yeorgi suppresses his heat as she persists.

"You look like shit. Smell like it too."

She's always had a talent for the low blow. She enjoys mocking him, preying on his self-esteem. Still, he's bound to his oath; to keep his cool.

Katarina senses her dagger missed the mark. Moving away, she lights a cigarette. She inhales deeply, then blows a smoke ring.

"So, why are you here? You got my payment?"

"I wanna see Trinket."

Katarina looks back at him, incredulous.

"You think she's awake at this…?"

"I won't wake her. I just wanna see her. Kiss her goodbye."

"Goodbye…!"

She catches herself. Of course, it's goodbye. She shoots him a bitter glare.

"How could you do this to us, you…"

"I'm sorry. You gotta understand. The Administration…"

"Don't…!"

She holds up a hand.

"Just don't. I don't need your politics right now."

She turns her back to him and takes another drag on the cigarette.

"As always, you bow to your hot head. No thought to consequences. No thought to nobody else. No thought to me." Then, as an afterthought, "… or Trinket."

Chastened, Yeorgi hangs his head. He knows she's right.

"Just let me see her, please, and I'll go."

Katarina turns back to him, snapping.

"The Beige could be here any minute."

"And they'll accuse you of abetting if you keep howling like a cat."

His barb hits the mark and catches Katarina

short.

How could it have come to this? She only looked for men who wanted to party. Before Yeorgi, she had her choice of high rollers. Married men with money who wanted sex on the side. She knew the game, and she didn't care. They took her places. High-end hotels with decent food. Trips to Paris even. Each told the other what they wanted to hear. None of it was true, but it was about good times. She knew she was a stunner. Still is, goddamn it. But now, saddled with a kid, no high roller wants her. How did she end up with a man of no means? And a radical; someone who's so angry at the world that he built a bomb. How in God's name did he learn to build a bomb? It's that goddam Sasha and the others who hang with him. Now this.

Broken and broke.

Looking at this pathetic man; her big mistake. If she turned him in, she'd be a hero.

After enduring so much, Yeorgi can read her eyes, her mulling betrayal.

"Just let me see Trinket and I'll go."

"Trinket. It's always, Trinket…."

It's the only thing that keeps her in the power position at this moment. Not her fine looks. Not sexual prowess. Trinket.

She takes another drag on the cigarette and blows out a long, thin line of smoke.

"And payments?"

Stunned, Yeorgi stares back at her, his

mouth agape. The Beige could barge in any minute. His life could end, and this bullshit is where she goes.

"Are you kidding me...?"

"Not."

Yeorgi struggles to tamp the fire inside.

"I'll get you money. Somehow. One way or another."

"You better."

"Or you could get off your fat ass and get a job!"

What he feared happens. His anger erupts.

The straw snaps.

Katarina plants herself, arms crossed.

"Get out."

"Trinket...."

Katarina won't have it. She rages at him.

"Get the hell out I said...!"

From the bedroom, a child wakens.

"Momma...?"

Yeorgi rushes towards the sound of the voice.

"Now look what you've...."

Katarina steps between him and the bedroom door and shrieks.

"Get the fuck out, I said!"

Yeorgi backhands her, knocking her to the ground. Bleeding at the lip, Katarina stares up at him, venom in her eyes. She stumbles towards the door leading to the hall.

"Help...! Somebody....!"

Yeorgi pushes the bedroom door open, peering into darkness.

Trinket, frail and malnourished, sits up in bed; torn from sleep, rubbing her eyes, surprised at what she sees.

"Daddy...?"

"Hi, baby...."

He wants to go to her. Hold her. Kiss her one last time. But it's too late.

Katarina has fled to the hallway outside the flat and cries out...

"Help! Help! Somebody...!"

Doors open. People step into the hall in their nightclothes.

Inside the flat, Yeorgi takes one last look at Trinket: tears in his eyes.

"Bye baby...."

In the outer hall, people rush to Katarina's aid.

Wailing...

Sobbing...

Horse tears.

Yeorgi bolts across the living room to the window, ripping at the shabby window shade. Crawling out, he hangs from the sill.

Voices in the flat...

Footsteps.

He releases his grip, dropping to the concrete. A shock of pain shoots up his leg as his ankle buckles under him.

From her window, Katarina watches him

run away, limping.

"You better run, you coward."

Her words echo through the empty street as Yeorgi passes through a shaft of light, disappearing into darkness.

"Coward...!"

***

Sasha, amid hypnotizing flames which have sprung up around him...

Surely, he's in hell...

The town he flees, his once safe harbour, is burning to the ground...

Firefighters, no longer able to ward off what had started in the bush miles away...

That which now sweeps through streets, consuming houses; turns the school, the playground, every single shop, and even The Town Hall to ash.

He'd joined the flow of others fleeing the fire. Now he stands next to his malfunctioning car on a road amid flames.

It must be his end.

The heat weakens him. The smoke dizzies him. Impending death. Resignation.

Then a wild deer darts past, determined to live.

Snapping to, Sasha joins the battle, following the deer, running along the highway, inhaling the searing heat. Staggering. Near collapse.

Then fate.

A truck breaks through the smoke. Screeches to a halt.

A woman at the wheel.

From behind the window glass, she motions.

Sasha, feeling a deer's life-force, leaps into the back of the truck.

She. Full throttle. Determined to outrun the inferno.

He. Wrapping his jacket around his head to inhale less smoke.

Her worried eyes in the rear-view mirror, taking in the stranger. Fearing that, at any minute, he may combust.

In the seat next to her, a terrified boy, six or seven, peering at Sasha through the rear window; his mummified head, wrapped.

On and on until, finally, escape from the flames…

A long stretch of road ahead.

The woman pulls off to the side, along with so many others, to look back; to take in the glow on the far horizon, their lost town.

To cough up char. Breathe air that doesn't scorch the lungs…

To embrace loved ones. Shed tears. Understand the loss.

Everything they carry is what they now own.

The newly displaced. Refugees, flowing

towards nearby towns, banking on kindness, an open door, sustenance.

Sasha looks toward the woman. The saint.

"You saved my life…."

She holds out her hand to him.

"Marta…."

Sasha, his face blackened from the smoke, hopefully unrecognizable as a fugitive. He holds out his hand to her and spouts the first alias that comes to mind.

"Robert…."

Marta looks at the boy next to her, making shy at first, his eyes now widening, astonished.

"Do you hear that, sweetie? This man has the same name as you. Robert."

***

Henry slips dark glasses on to avoid the glare of the morning sun.

Eyes on the road, he looks for an off-ramp leading to a crossroad leading to a hidden country lane leading to a link. A Safehouse. And a charging-station for the car…

Respite…

Part of a chain of sorts, strung out across the country…

The rebellious are everywhere.

Earlier, he was mindful of a drone overhead, monitoring traffic. He remained calm until it left. He's glad Jack wasn't aware. Panicked.

He looks over at him, asleep in the passenger

seat. He had another dreadful night. Ever since William, he cannot find peaceful sleep; kept awake by self-blame, as if he could've stopped The Administration from taking him. He says he should've fought until death, but Henry has never blamed him. Who knows how he himself might've reacted had he been home when they came? Had a gun at his head, demanding he brave death for a lost cause, saving someone viewed as flawed, unworthy, a drag on a dying planet, something he and Jack are approaching as they near sixty.

It's the people on the street who look at him with pity that Henry can't stand; knowing that his time is soon; his imminent Eveningsong...

A reminder of their own.

William's Eveningsong is what drove him and Jack apart. Two men who'd loved one another since the beginning of time; loved a man-child they'd raised from his early breaths.

Henry consoling...

Jack, inconsolable...

Both grieving...

Until finally, a letter left leaning against a cup on the kitchen table... "I'm leaving."

Henry searching...

Finding...

Begging Jack to come home.

"Forget me, Henry. Take care of yourself."

Watching him slip ever deeper into darkness...

But never giving up on him. Ever.

Keeping track of his movements from place to place, from one rooming house to another.

Knowing he had settled in shabby rooms above a hardware store, near a bakery.

Finally, approaching him one last time. Needing him to hear the urgency.

Sensing there was hope when he learned Jack had no phone; was trying to disappear from databases. Knowing that beneath the wretchedness, there was a belief in living; in carrying on, even though Jack couldn't see it himself.

Henry cranks the wheel and turns onto a country road leading to an overgrown lane the rebels told him of in coded messages; a lane overhung with shady boughs, narrow enough that bushes along its sides caress the car, leading to a Safehouse in the middle of nowhere.

The bumping of the car over the rutted lane wakens Jack.

He, confused at first, rubbing eyes that opened to a world that is less real than the dream world….

"Where are we…?"

"Someplace safe. We can rest here and charge the car."

But as they approach the end of the lane and an open field, they see no house. Only a pile of broken bricks. Rubble that was once a house, bulldozed.

A sign: '*By Order of The Administration.*'

On a nearby post, a camera aimed at the head of the lane.

At once, Henry throws the car into reverse, speeding along the lane backwards; branches, scraping against the sides of the car, clawing at it, as if to hold them back, capture them. Then swerving back onto the crossroad to the ramp and to the main highway.

Away, before the drones come.

CHAPTER 4

The Senior.
In his office. Alone…
It's late…
A single lamp burning…
He; elbows on the desk, chin cupped in his hands, contemplative…
He likes the quietude…
Minutes pass…
Putting puzzle pieces together in his mind, there's something wrong with the picture.
He rises from the desk and walks to the glass wall overlooking the colour-coded work-pods. The four-to-midnight shift is clicking keyboards and scanning screens. Taking in details. Processing.
Green for finance…
Yellow for career…
Blue, family…
Education, black…
Notable achievements, brown…
Red for politics…
And all imaginable hues in between,

signifying the most subtle affiliations.

The Administration trusts everyone who works for it. But it trusts most, those who work in the red pods. The Senior has vetted each one of them to form an elite unit. They're able to draw together elements from any other colour groups to create complete profiles of anyone in the city. Even him. Able to connect with databases in other cities around the world in aid of detecting and tracking rebellion.

But in recent times, something in its systems has gone wrong.

It has never been perfect. The Senior recalls an incident where The Administration staged a raid on an apartment in Chinatown, only to discover the person they wanted to arrest had moved out the day before, and new tenants occupied the space.

A lapse in the lime-coloured residential/real estate pods.

As a result, smashed doors and windows left innocent people terrorized; left them untrusting of anyone in a beige uniform. More important, The Administration lost valuable hours. The suspect escaped.

Almost.

Facial recognition found him in a neighbouring town, and The Beige captured him.

But something is different this time.

The Administration knows those responsible for bombing The Amphorium. But synapses in big data make improper connections, and the bombers have escaped.

Days have passed and, so far, nothing. That's never the case. No facial recognition hits, no financial transactions recorded: vehicle charging stations, restaurants, food stores. Nothing. They're bartering or using cash.

More likely, they've connected with The Underground. The Administration knows it exists. Under such a regime, it's bound to. Where The Senior subscribes to the ultimate rule; the survival of humankind, no matter what cost, others view the regime's methods as dictatorial. Even inhumane.

So far, The Administration has not destroyed the entire underground network. Each time they find a cell; others pop up somewhere else. Attempts at infiltration are so far ineffective.

From time to time, their infinite databases congeal the facts and lead them to a single cell or two, which they bulldoze right away. Then they post a warning sign: '*By Order of The Administration.*' They publicize executions of insurgents as a deterrent, but rebels still exist. Sometimes, they escape.

Looking now over the red pods, he wonders where the bug lay. Is it a flaw in the software, the computer's grey matter? Or is the bug a person? Is it/he/she housed in the red pods? The bug could seed itself in any of the colours. A bug in the most mundane of details could affect everything else up the chain, making what purports to be the most relevant, irrelevant.

Just because one puzzle piece might have a similar shape as another doesn't mean it belongs in that place. Similar-shaped pieces wrongly positioned could cause a distorted picture.

The Senior returns to his desk and sits...

Fingers drumming.

He looks at the clock on his screen. Past eleven. Cherise and the girls will be asleep.

Fingers still drumming.

***

Bateman.

In bed with Ginni...

Naked...

He rolls over and spoons into her body. His wayward hand cups a breast.

Ginni squirms.

"Twice last night. Haven't you had enough?"

Bateman's morning erection. Engorged. Painful.

"Apparently not."

"Then take care of it yourself. I've got to get ready for work."

She slides out of bed, gathering up clothes strewn here and there as she pads into the bathroom.

The automatic shower turns on as she steps under the nozzle. She hates Bateman's shower. If she moves too far left or right, the flow of water stops.

Conservation.

"You've got to adjust the sensor on your shower."

From the bedroom. "What…?"

Louder. "The goddamn shower! It's too sensitive."

Back in the bedroom, Bateman lights a cigarette and fondles himself.

"I'll take care of it."

From the bathroom. "What…?"

Louder. "I said, I'll take care of it!"

Crawling out of bed, cigarette dangling from his lips, he slips into yesterday's underwear, stowing his erection. He steps up to a window and gazes out.

Acres and acres of barley fields.

He thinks of Lila Wong; the long black hair that had landed on his sleeve the other day. There'd be no complaints from her around his early morning urge. He's convinced of it. He doubts Ginni would care less if he got passive-aggressive right now; tells her he has feelings for Lila. From the outset, she said she wasn't ready to commit to just one guy, *"Let's keep it casual."* Easy for her to say when he's always at the ready whenever she feels the urge. For him, not a day passes. Once or twice a month satisfies her. At least with him. He wonders if she has other men in thralldom.

Looking out at the rising sun, he sees it shaping up to be another swelter.

He longs for the day he can leave this Podunk town—one road in, one road out—but because of population migration inland, it's growing, the same as so many other towns and villages that used to go by in a blink, even at a slow drive. Still, he longs for The Administration to elevate him to headquarters in the city, to where the real action is. That won't happen soon if more RV incidents involving innocent people and children happen. Still, they can't blame him. He and his team went with the information they got. The Administration are the screw-ups. Right there and then, he decides he'll no longer trust incoming intelligence. He'll scrutinize it more deeply, ask more questions.

From the bathroom: "Goddamn it...!"

Bateman smirks as he hears the water turn off, then on. Off, then on again.

The only reason they sent him to this town in the first place is to train rookies. It's out of the way, and being rookies, they can do less damage. It's a source of consternation that Alistair Goodwin, with whom he graduated from The Academy, is, even now, at headquarters.

Mind you, Bateman's job isn't irrelevant. The highway through town is one which those fleeing Eveningsong use to travel to The Haven; a fabled place they believe lay somewhere in the mountains on the other side of the country.

An Eden...

A safe place...

Free…

A stronghold defended by weaponized rebels, so they claim.

As far as Bateman knows, it doesn't exist. But that doesn't stop people from trying to reach it. He's lost count of the number of suspicious vehicles he and his team have stopped. Suspicious because the occupants weigh them down with a life's worth of belongings and provisions. And sometimes stowed in the trunk, a grandma or sick uncle long past their due date; past Eveningsong. Potential draws on resources.

They'll never learn.

The RV incident was irksome. Instead of capturing five dangerous bombers—great for his résumé—he confronted a terrified family. He hates when it involves children. They lose respect for the uniform. Their trauma might make them rebels-in-waiting. And even though it was The Administration that screwed up, it's still a blot on his record. At least that's the way he views it.

Ginni steps out of the bathroom in full uniform. Her hair swept up into a tight knot on the top of her head.

"Wearing a uniform each day is a good thing. You don't have to make the walk of shame the next morning."

With that, she heads to the door.

"See you at the office."

She wiggles her fingers at him over her shoulder and leaves without even a goodbye-peck on the cheek.

Bateman harrumphs.

He takes one last drag on the cigarette as he slides a hand into his briefs.

***

Alistair Goodwin, dreaming.
William's hands reaching out. Grasping...
"Dadda...! Dadda...!"
Alistair restraining him...
Jack's plea. "Don't...."
Bateman forcing Jack to his knees. Holding him...
"Please."
Bateman's gun to Jack's head...
William, crying out...
"Dadda...!"
Jack's tears...
Bateman's demand...
"Make the choice."
"No, please...!"

Alistair, in the real world, thrashing, kicking through knotted sheets. Bateman's voice reverberating in the ether.

"Choose...!"

Alistair sits bolt upright in his bed, gasping. In the darkness, dream images pixilate. Voices echo and dissolve. He's trapped between the dreamworld and the real until...

A bedside table...

A chair...

The framed butterflies on the opposite wall...

The world solidifying. Dream images melting, but not the emotion...

Distress.

Alistair disentangles himself from the twisted sheets and stumbles out of bed, drenched in sweat.

Staggering to a window, he peers through unfocused eyes at the cityscape. He pushes the window open and sticks his head out, taking in deep breaths to quell his racing heart. He assures himself that the air is indeed sweeter than just a couple of years ago, fewer particulates. The Administration's measures are working.

Still, the dream haunts him. It has, ever since he studied the profiles of two of the alleged bombers: Jack Parnell and Henry Chagall.

Horrid memories triggered.

***

Veronica Lake is serving today.

It's Wednesday, so Alistair orders the usual French toast.

He wonders if the doppelgänger even knows who Veronica Lake was. Ah yes. There's the black-and-white photo of her in a grouping on the wall...

Part of the décor...

Celebrities from a movieland long gone.

Alistair loves old movies, especially the black and white ones. Back then, there was a well-defined good and evil. The villains wore black hats and the heroes, white. Then there followed a different era when it became muddied. People were more attuned to nuance. That was before Reckoning, before the earth rebelled. Nowadays, it's reverted to black and white. Those who believe in Eveningsong are the good guys. Those who defy it are outlaws. He sees the irony in his beige uniform. It's a non-colour. Neither a black hat nor a white hat. Neither good nor bad. He wonders about the significance of that thought.

He finds it difficult to set aside last night's horrible dream.

"Dadda...! Dadda...!"

To deflect, he focuses on Veronica's ass, swaying from side to side as she glides away from him after pouring piping hot acorn coffee. As she picks up his French toast from the kitchen pass-through and returns, he wants to ask her if she likes her job. Or is it what's available to her—a wannabe movie star waiting for her big break? Imitating Veronica Lake, with her hair draped over one eye until movieland discovers her at last. If it worked for Veronica, it could work for her. Or is she a woman scorned? Jilted and now struggling to make ends meet. There's a hint of weary cynicism in that one exposed eye. As she sets out Alistair's food, he suppresses the question. He knows she won't answer. It's not part of the script. Soon she moves on to the other tables, leaving Alistair to face last night's horrifying dream alone.

It isn't just a dream. They're true events, recalled. Bateman held a gun to Jack Parnell's head. He *did* yell at Alistair to "keep the *re*tard back." He *did* make Jack Parnell chose. It wasn't a matter of the man-child's life or his. It was William's life *and* his. Either Jack allowed them to take the *re*tard away or die with him right there and then. William's fate was Eveningsong. Also, for Jack. It was for the greater good and the survival of humankind. Jack Parnell's choice could delay his own Eveningsong by years, but not the man-child. The Administration considered his mongolism an infirmity; a draw on everyone else. They had to end him. It's the law.

Sipping the steaming brew, Alistair wonders why he can't let it go.

Jack Parnell made his choice. He saved himself. Simple as that.

Looking around the cafe, he sees the old man again. The same one he saw before at 'The Un-Greasy Spoon.' Only this time, the man doesn't look away. He stares back at Alistair, unblinking, eyes penetrating, reading his thoughts…

No fear this time.

Since the bombing of The Amphorium, there's less fear in people's eyes. Instead, one that says, "A saviour has arrived…."

For reasons Alistair can't fathom, an image pops into his head. High school basketball, the coach screaming, "No 'I' in team." More remembrance as he pours syrup onto his French toast. His Fraternity, pledging. He; held in place while the gang pour a bucket of their combined piss over him. Surviving it, unlike other Pledges who head for the door. Unlike them, Alistair became elevated; they made him a brother. He remembers it now as strong as the disturbing dream. And how when his turn came, he visited the same humiliation on new Pledges, his subordinates. Added his piss.

Later in business, he'd done the same, adopting the requisite grey flannel suit and striped tie of a junior executive on the rise; his passive-aggressive humiliation of those who didn't conform, forcing them to the door. And when that fell apart, and he joined The Beige, how inoculated he'd already become. By then, how ready he was to follow the dominant rule. It was easy to believe in Eveningsong. Relinquish the "I" so the team could survive. He and Bateman were side by side at The Academy. Alistair can't help wondering now why The Administration elevated him instead of Bateman; someone who will hold a gun to a man's head and make him choose.

Having downed the last bit of his breakfast, Veronica presents the bill to Alistair with a flip of her hair, revealing a second captivating eye. He pays, adding a generous tip as thanks for a glimpse.

Looking back across the room, he sees the old man still watching him; an insubordinate grin, as if he is a Pledge who opts for the door.

Alistair's chair scrapes the floor as he

rises. He approaches the man and holds out a demanding hand to him. "Papers…."

Silent, the old man slides his identity card out of his wallet and, without question, presents it to the man in beige.

Alistair scrutinizes it. "By my calculation, you're nearing sixty."

The old man fixes his remorseless eyes on Alistair, the grin unrelenting. "Not long now, I guess…."

Alistair looms over him, willing the old man to look away. Wishing for it.

But the old man won't break his glare.

Fuming, Alistair flips the identity card onto the tabletop. He turns and slams through the swinging glass door, loosening its hinges.

***

Five-year-old identical twins, Prunella and Rosie, jump onto the bed, jolting The Senior out of a sound sleep.

"Daddy! Daddy…!"

They crawl over him like kittens in a basket. Their little fingers walk up his face and pry his eyes open.

"Wake up. Wake up…!"

Cherise runs into the room, shooing them away.

"Let daddy sleep for God's sake. Monsters!"

The kittens transform into fiends and growl.

The Senior springs to his feet on top of

the bed, looming over them; a giant ogre with a tremendous roar.

High-pitched screams from the mini monsters as they scurry out of the room.

The Senior chuckles and flops back onto the bed as Cherise sidles up next to him.

"Sorry, love. The little rats got away from me."

"I should get out of bed."

"It's Saturday. You should sleep."

"A mug of hot chicory and I'll be ready to go."

Cherise curls deeper into him.

"You were in late again."

"Lots to figure out."

"The bombing, you mean. It's been days. Still nothing?"

"We'll resolve it."

Cherise shoots him a considered look. They've been together long enough for her to know when he's worried. Still, she knows she won't get the details out of him. He keeps so much secret, including personal information. He's always been an intense, private man-of-few-words. When she first met him, she found the "man-of-mystery thing" compelling. But even after so many years together, she feels she doesn't know him. Still, her love is genuine. She's never been clingy, believing the day will come when he opens himself up to her and she's willing to wait. She gives him a peck on the lips and crawls off the bed. Crossing the room, she pushes the drapes aside, letting in sunlight.

The Senior squints and holds up his hands. "The light. Oh, the light. I'm melting…!"

As always, Cherise laughs. It's an old joke.

She cocks an ear.

"It's too quiet. The monsters are up to something."

Her voice trails off as she makes her way out of the room and along the hall.

"Okay monsters. What's happening…?"

Distant giggles and squeals.

Laying back, The Senior reflects on how he enjoys the giggles and squeals and how lucky he is. A woman who loves him, and Prunella and Rosie. He's aware that, behind his back, people disapprove of a family with two children. There's an unspoken rule nowadays that couples limit offspring to one. Or even none. Especially those in The Administration, who should set an example. When he and Cherise learned twins were on the way, subtle people implied they should abort one of the pair. He and Cherise just couldn't bring themselves to do it. How does one choose? But it's only an unspoken rule. And he knows that, being a Senior in The Administration, those around him are unwilling to press the point on hypocrisy.

His job affords his family a spacious section in one of the most elite mansions in the city. During Reckoning, hundreds of such houses went up in flames. Once The Administration set its Law of Each-one-for-Everyone, they subdivided surviving luxury properties into multi-family dwellings. The theory is that such a scheme will save on resources. At first, they allotted families' space based on the number of its occupants. Lately, they've added rank to the list of qualifications.

A subtle hierarchy has arisen. No one says it aloud, but people sense it. For instance, living in a subdivided mansion is a step up from a subdivided bungalow in a lesser neighbourhood. And more elite than an apartment building in an even lesser neighbourhood that didn't need subdividing. Even within a mansion, there's an unspoken pecking order. The Senior lives on the first floor. People consider that prime real estate, as opposed to an upper floor. Residents on a first floor don't have to climb stairs. And although it goes against the law of Each-one-for-Everyone, it hasn't taken long for members of The Administration—or those with a connection inside it—to snap up the most preferred spaces…

Including Elizabeth Lowell.

She's one of the alleged bombers and she occupied the third-floor garret in the same house as The Senior.

She's since disappeared.

The Senior thought he knew her well enough. Ironic that it was he who offered himself as a reference when she applied for residency, two flights up in the attic space. The reason she offered for wanting to live there impressed him. She said that, instead of living on a first floor in a lesser neighbourhood, it's better to live in a garret at the best address. To The Senior, that mindset showed ambition.

She was a low-level functionary in The Administration, working in the sky-blue section, documenting the public's preferences for various toiletries. But The Senior sensed potential in her. She has a quick mind and an incredible eye for detail with a knack for intricate coding. She had often undersold herself, which The Senior considers a potential weakness in anyone. Overcoming humbleness makes one a candidate for the red level.

It's humiliating to think that duping him was easy for her. He now questions her reasons for living upstairs, near a Senior in The Administration. He questions each word he ever spoke to her, not only at headquarters, but during their comings and goings at the mansion. The more he thinks, the more he builds a convincing case. Elizabeth Lowell is the bug.

After linking her to the bombing, The Administration ransacked the garret looking for shreds of evidence. She planned her escape well in advance and had sanitized the place beforehand. She had destroyed paper files and removed her technology. There was no computer to analyze. She may have taken it with her. If she ever logs on, they can track her, but so far nothing. It's as though she and her compatriots ceased to exist. Everything has disappeared: on-line profiles, pictures. Not only for her, but for the others involved in the bombing as well. Even Elizabeth's encrypted employee file has disappeared. Until now, such a vanishing act was unheard of, if not impossible, in a connected world. Indeed, soon after the bombing, The Administration scrambled to find a hard copy photograph they could scan and post to media. It's frustrating that whatever they post online of her, and the others pixelates and then it vanishes. The Administration has taken to sending out hard copies of what they now call The Group-of-Five to pin on corkboards at Administration offices, and on lampposts and the sides of buildings across the country.

His hope is that committed loyalists will recognize the bombers and turn them over to authorities.

***

Night...

A shaft of dim solar light fans out from a lamppost, illuminating a fresh poster plastered on the wall of a barbershop. The poster depicts the faces of the wanted. And it replaces an earlier one which somebody, defying the law, obliterated with black spray-paint.

So far, the bombers have gone uncaptured. Cells known as The Fringe have arisen across the entire country to support them. To The Fringe, The Group-of-Five is a cause célèbre, standing for an opposing view. To them, Eveningsong is inhumane and reflects a corrupt administration which has tilted towards dictatorship.

Those who know history see a familiar pattern. No matter how egalitarian a regime starts out, soon an elite ascends and separates themselves from those they view as "common." They command privileges above others. When questioned, they assert their power. It's become far too easy to disappear anyone for illegitimate reasons, under the guise of the law of Each-one-for-Everyone.

It's ironic that such actions provoke more rebellion, even in small ways…

Such as black paint.

It could run amok. Once again, there could be anarchy. That cannot happen.

The Administration has convinced the vast majority to believe in the laws of Each-one-for-Everyone and Eveningsong. To them, The Group-of-Five are traitors to the cause. The Fringe are no less a threat to the survival of humankind than the Amphorium bombers themselves. So, The Administration has no choice but to mete out justice. Even death, for which is—on the surface at least—a minor infraction.

As a result, Bateman lays in wait this night in his village for one or more to appear from the darkness and vandalize the new poster. Night after night he's waited. Still nothing. Yet, he's willing to bide time…

Especially after the RV incident.

Hoping to get back into the good graces of The Administration, he's concealed himself in a darkened doorway with an unobstructed view of the lamppost and the poster. He's bent on capturing at least one of The Fringe.

He considered including more of his team, but his instincts tell him he's dealing with a lone actor. Besides, why share the glory? Even if there are two or even three of them, he believes with his pistol at the ready, he can take what comes. So, make it two or three.

Glory, glory, glory....

Wait.

Is that movement in the alley...?

Yes.

At last, a slender figure wearing black from head to toe, a balaclava obscuring his face from a nearby recognition camera.

Silent...

Furtive, with the subtlest of movements.

Bateman wonders how long the other man has been there, surveying the scene. Was he aware of Bateman before Bateman was aware of him? Has Bateman himself moved too often in his darkened doorway, giving himself away? He mustn't move now. If he reacts too soon, he'll blow the whole thing. He must wait for the other man to make his move; to slip out of the alley. He must catch him in the act, otherwise there's no case.

It doesn't take long.

Soon, the man in black darts out of the

alley and, with lightening speed, sprays a large "X" across the poster.

Bateman makes his move. He leaps from concealment.

"STOP!"

Startled, the man in black bolts back into the alley, making a run for it.

Bateman gives chase.

The man topples a trash can, tripping up Bateman.

He hits the ground with a great thud.

"Son of a bitch…!"

Now angrier and even more determined, he springs to his feet and pursues the man, who rounds the back corner of the barbershop, out of sight.

With trepidation, Bateman approaches the corner and peers around it.

A blast of spray-paint to the eyes.

Bateman falls back, yelping.

"Mother fuck…!"

He hears running footsteps and the rattle of a chain-link fence.

Wiping his eyes, he squints through a blur seeing the man in black, his pant leg now ensnared on a wire fence.

Bateman leaps onto him.

The man, who has freed himself, kicks Bateman in the face.

Bateman grapples with him.

They fall from the fence, hitting the

pavement, hard.

Flailing, the man in black connects a fist with Bateman's jaw.

Bateman has had enough.

He winds up and coldcocks the man, knocking him unconscious.

Breathless, he rolls the man over and sits astride his chest.

He snatches at the balaclava, revealing the face of a handsome young man.

"Why, you're just a kid…."

He recognizes him as the seventeen-year-old son of the local mayor.

CHAPTER 5

An abandoned barn...
Dilapidated...
Once trim and well-kept, now decomposing...
Wood graying...
Stone foundation crumbling...
Fragile doors falling off their hinges...

Holes left in the roof where fierce winds ripped away shingles and scattered them across the field. Never restored to their rightful place. There's nobody there to do it. The former farmer and his wife were childless. There's no younger generation left behind to take over the farm and make it run.

Now, only shafts of dusty sunlight streaming through the rotting rafters, clinging to the motes. The tangy smell of rusting iron tools: a scythe, a saw, rakes, and hoes. Symbols of someone's history, hanging on nails, hammered into a wall. Precisely placed by a well-organized and methodical man. Left untouched after years.

The farmer and his wife—two souls that shared a life as one before aging into Eveningsong. Now, what's left of their history is a toppling barn, and the charred remains of a nearby farmhouse, burned to the ground as an act of defiance.

Local lore has it that, on their shared sixtieth birthday, May nineteenth, The Administration found the couple seated together on rickety kitchen chairs in front of the smoking ruins. Waiting. At which point, The Beige took them to the nearest Amphorium, and, after forty years together, the farmer and his wife offered each other a last kiss. Unflinching, they held hands throughout a straightforward infusion until death. Then flames engulfed their bodies; turned them to ash as if they were an obsolete farmhouse.

Forgotten now; their act of defiance is only a footnote in a database. Except that, to this day, wildflowers from seeds strewn by the farmer's wife, now sprout among the ruins and spread across the yard to the barn, and beyond to the fields where cabbages once grew.

Soon, climate refugees will arrive on this land, and with the aid of The Administration, build a neighbourhood. Imagine. Block after block of small prefabricated mini houses towed in and set atop pylons drilled into the verdant soil.

Squat...

Oblong shoe boxes...

Efficient and self-sustaining...

Solar panels on their roofs. Bio-degrading

toilets.

But until such time, only Jack Parnell and Henry Chagall, pushing the MINI Cooper up a rutted road towards the crumbling barn. The car's battery is now depleted.

Unaware of the history of this place or its future, they swing the barn's rickety doors open, scraping them along the ground, marking angel wings in the dust. They roll the MINI Cooper into the barn. It's unwise to abandon it at the side of the road. A drone will soon discover it. Relay images back to headquarters for cross-referencing. It could lead to the unraveling of their escape.

So, no. Best to keep the car and themselves out of sight.

Jack falls back against the car, exhausted. It isn't just because they had to push a defunct vehicle for a mile along a country road, and then across the field to the barn. It's everything. He and Henry have been on the road for days. Often travelling under cover of night. At other times, travelling on crowded highways to blend. But always a circuitous route, sometimes doubling back on themselves or ducking into a hidden spot in aid of ensuring no one's following them. It means they only advance short miles each day. If Henry's plan is to get them to The Haven, which they say is somewhere in the mountains on the other side of the country, at such a rate, it'll take months to get there.

To disguise himself, Henry has taken to

spraying a black dye into his silver hair, which only makes his startling blue eyes even bluer. And Jack has taken to wearing a baseball cap and dark glasses, which happily make him look younger. So far, they've evaded detection. Henry tells Jack that they have Elizabeth to thank for keeping facial recognition cameras from perceiving them. His explanation is befuddling because it has something to do with algorithms, and Jack was never good at algebra.

Jack slips off his T-shirt, using it to wipe perspiration dripping from his face and torso.

Henry takes in his fit body.

"You're still in great shape for someone your age."

"Don't, Henry…"

"It's not seduction. Take the compliment."

Their eyes lock briefly until Jack looks away.

"I swim three times a week."

"You're blushing…."

"You're doing that thing."

"What thing?"

Jack throws him a skeptical look and slips back into the shirt.

"So, what's our next move…?"

Henry takes off the neckerchief he wears and spreads it on the hood of the car. The first morning after their escape, he explained to Jack that the intricate, yet innocent-looking pattern imprinted on the neckerchief is an elaborate, encoded map. He himself developed it for the group, assigning a new symbol to each of the twenty-six letters of the alphabet and numbers zero through nine; each one committed to memory: a cross for the letter 'A', the sum symbol for the letter 'B', a circle for the letter 'C', etcetera. And a new symbol for numbers zero through nine.

The symbols and numbers, joined here and there with long and short lines, form a map of the entire country with locations for a string of Safehouses. Places such as the one The Administration had unfortunately discovered and bulldozed, making it impossible to recharge the car. It's why they find themselves in their current predicament, hiding in a tumbledown barn in the middle of nowhere with a non-operational MINI Cooper.

And there is oncoming rain.

Henry points at the map.

"The last town we passed through was Handlynde...."

Jack leans in to look.

"That's right."

Henry points, "The bulldozed Safehouse was there, which puts us here."

"Where's the next Safehouse?"

Henry points to another spot on the cloth map.

"Here. A place called Coal Town."

"An unfortunate name."

"I'll bet it's abandoned by now. Which makes it a good place for a Safehouse."

"How far…?"

Henry scrutinizes the symbols.

"Close to sixteen kilometres."

"We can't push the car sixteen kilometres!"

"We'll figure something out."

Jack looks up through the rafters. The sun no longer streams through the holes in the roof and the sky has turned grey.

"Rain's coming."

"Get the tent out. I'll whip up the grub."

Jack reaches into the back of the MINI Cooper and pulls out a solar knapsack, from which he extracts a cloth pouch the size of a notebook. Folded inside is a two-man tent made of thin silken fabric; shiny solar foil on one side, dull matte on the other. He spreads the fabric on the floor in a sheltered corner of the barn that he hopes will stay dry once the rain starts. Later, when he and Henry crawl into the giant pouch, their radiant body heat will inflate the tent into a tepee. With the solar foil facing inward, their reflected body heat will keep them warm. To cool the tent on hot days, the whole thing turns inside out causing the solar foil to, not only deflect the sun while absorbing its energy, but use that energy to charge a solar lamp to illuminate either the inside of the tent or a whole campsite.

Ingenious.

Come the day, it can charge a car battery.

Meanwhile, Henry removes another solar knapsack from the back of the car. Inside is a hotplate the knapsack has charged. As well, from the back of the car, he takes out basic cooking utensils, including a large aluminium pot with a domed lid. The pot is a magician's hat. Henry pulls out one thing after another: a couple of collapsible steamers along with two bowls, two plates, two cups and knives, forks, and spoons; all made from bamboo. Feeling wistful, Jack watches as Henry pours water into the pot, into which he empties a bag of dry vegetable soup mix. He then adds herbs and chili flakes from the grocery box to give it his personal zing. Then he places one plate on top of the pot, onto which he puts two freeze-dried biscuits. Once he places the domed lid on top of the pot and sets it on the hotplate, it'll create a convection oven which not only heats the soup but bakes the bread rolls.

In better days, on camping trips with William, Jack used to look on and marvel at how Henry created a full-course meal, from soup to dessert using only a camp stove, a single pot and a couple of bamboo steamers. He envisions Henry, tomorrow morning, whipping up a couple of impossibly tasty omelets using only egg and milk powders, along with dehydrated onion and bacon bits. That, along with piping hot chicory lovingly brewed in the magic pot.

More than acceptable for a couple of old tarts on the run.

The storm clouds roll in and the inside of the barn grows dim. Jack clicks on the solar lamp and together he and Henry dig into their meager but delicious meal. Their dinner music, the plaintive rumble of a far-off freight train.

Later, there's a deluge. Henry strips naked and stands in the rain, rinsing not only his body, but the dishes.

From inside the barn, Jack calls out.

"Come inside, Henry. You'll catch your death."

Henry peers into the darkened barn.

"Come *outside*, Jack. After so many days on the road, you stink."

Jack steps up to the barn door and looks out, his mouth curling into a cautious grin.

"This is definitely you in full seduction mode, Henry."

"Stop fighting me, Jack."

Finally, Jack gives in and strips. He stands in the rain, letting it stream over him.

After a thorough scrub, he and Henry duck back into the barn to their dry corner. They huddle together inside the fabric pouch, waiting for their body heat to return.

Soon, the conical tent inflates.

***

Zero and one. Ones and zeros.

True or false. False or true.

Changing a one to a zero in the code can make what is true, false. Or make what is false, now true.

Blue eyes become green.

Black hair becomes blonde.

The measurement between the crook of the nose and its tip is no longer correct. The distance between the eyes, the shape of the lip, the cleft in the chin become the face of someone else. Facial recognition becomes disordered. The Administration sends its officers to arrest John Smith but find only Mary Jones.

A zero or a one in the code can create lies.

Bugs in a network made weak because it's centralized.

No doubt a clever whiz will untangle it. It surprises Elizabeth they haven't yet. Still, she knows that once the genius corrects a bug in the chain, her code reconfigures and creates another one.

On and on it goes.

Grinning at the thought of it, Elizabeth speeds along the highway through the pitch-black night. She glimpses herself in the rear-view mirror. It's a correct image. Ones and zeros can't alter it. And since she's gone on the run, the image in the mirror is her only company.

For two years, she hid her brilliance under a self-effacing facade, which upper management interpreted as weak; making her unworthy of promotion out of her pale blue pod. Truth-be-told, she didn't want a promotion. Instead, she gave the impression of someone dedicated to her meager mandate: *"Making the world a better place by cataloging preferences for toiletries to help avoid depletion of resources."* As far as upper management knew, that mundane directive satisfied her. But, unknown to them, during her off-time, she developed a code which—when the time came—she planted in the systems' brain to aid her escape, and that of her compatriots.

After the horrors of Reckoning, the new administration had developed projects that benefit humankind: most notably a worldwide electrical grid powered by a combination of solar, wind and tidal forces to augment nuclear power. And they have forced electric and hydrogen powered vehicles. But, even now, people consider Elizabeth's electric vehicle outmoded because of the resources wasted to make and then dispose of lithium batteries.

Fossil fuels should be next to irrelevant. However, powerful oil interests seeking profit continue to drill, and wells continue to pump.

The Administration has developed new products using bamboo, jute, banana leaves and cannabis to replace plastics. The earth is rebelling. Near extinction focuses the mind. That threat has unleashed an enormous burst of creativity. A new enlightenment. The adage says, "Necessity is the mother of invention." Innovative minds increasingly leave non-renewables out of their inventions, capitalizing on renewables only. What has followed is heady. Logical minds see problems as opportunities: How does one build a complete vehicle out of renewables only? It hasn't happened yet, but Elizabeth sees it on the horizon. And only because the earth continually speaks up, saying, enough is enough.

But none of that's the problem.

A dark side has appeared within The Administration, leading to deceptive abuses of the law of Each-one-for-Everyone. To Elizabeth, it's no surprise that an elite class has risen from the masses. It always does. Like prominent theorists, she believes that, even if an entire population starts out with the same opportunities, with enough time and subterfuge, less than one percent of the population will still end up with ninety percent of the wealth and power. It's not right, but it's true. And has been throughout history.

But, for Elizabeth and her cohorts, even that's not the problem.

It's Eveningsong.

Forced death.

What started out as altruistic sacrifice for the good of everyone has become a way to disappear people without cause. Or with "manufactured cause." Nowadays, so-called enemies of the people have too easily disappeared because they hold an opposing view, or because someone in the elite wants something they have: wealth or political power. Or even something absurd, such as a better address.

The Beige, a force The Administration initially set up to protect the people, has become complicit. And in its complicity, fiercer. Terrorizing. Elizabeth has seen from the inside as more of those with extreme views rise to the top and bring into The Beige those who match their views. Now, The Beige are attacking dogs instead of protectors. Each of her co-conspirators has suffered at their hands; Henry Chagall and his spouse, for instance. Their intellectually challenged son, who was uncomprehending of what was happening to him as they dragged him away. And Elizabeth's own father—a man with a brilliant mind—whom The Beige shot in the street for sport, then conspired to claim he resisted Eveningsong.

He did not.

But The Administration wanted to silence him because of secret information about them, which he'd uncovered.

His murder led Elizabeth to become complicit in the bombing of The Amphorium.

From the darkness, a road sign in the headlights: SHAFTSBURY → 26. The Safehouse Elizabeth seeks is there. Following the arrow, she cranks the wheel, taking a fork in the road. For the past half-hour, her eyes have strained from fatigue. It's time she gets off the main highway.

She thinks of the others in the group, hoping they're safe tonight, especially Yeorgi, who's the most anarchic. And being volatile, he's the most likely to blow his cover. If she's done her job well, and Yeorgi can hold his temper, The Beige will have yet to arrest any of them. Unless old-fashioned wanted posters right out of the Wild West will lead to the capture of those now labelled enemies of the people.

Finally arriving on the outskirts of Shaftsbury, she slows the car. She pulls off to the side of the road under a streetlamp and unravels a neckerchief wrapped around her wrist. It's an identical map to the ones each member of the group has. She spreads it on her lap in the dim light and deciphers.

The Safehouse is on the other side of town. The Beige will be on patrol, so she must continue with caution. A lone car driving through mostly deserted streets at night will stand out. Still, she has no choice. The car's battery is running low on energy, and so is she. Balling up the neckerchief, she crams it into the pocket of her cardigan and drives on.

***

Yeorgi.
In his black pickup…
Parked beneath an overpass…
It's the only safe place.

A sudden downburst. Winds strong enough to smash a forest; to roll his truck over and over if luck wasn't with him. Unlike the driver of a compact sedan behind him on the highway. Luck against him and unable to make it to the underpass in time, the wind dragged his car away.

Him inside, tumbling…
Breaking…
Bones cracking…
Without question, he's dead.

Others, more fortunate, crammed into the tunnel, praying for subsidence. Fearing the explosive wind might suck them away too; strew them across the landscape as though they are children's toys.

Yeorgi has never felt so powerless, so annoyed.

To have fought; taken a stand and set a bomb, then to have fled. To have made it this far, only to meet an ignoble death; have angry nature take him. Yet, that's everyone's fear nowadays. Nature outraged. Vengeful.

Fires…
Floods…
Devastating winds…
Ice…
And then, immediate swelter.

Privation of the masses, moving away from the coast to the centre of the country. Believing that it's safer there. Instead, finding nature everywhere, making her case.

Yeorgi rubs his aching knee, then slides a hand to his swollen ankle. It's yet to heal from the strain when he dropped from Katarina's window to the concrete sidewalk. The pain is near unbearable.

A sudden gust vacuums through the

underpass.

Yeorgi's truck rattles.

He grips the steering wheel expecting any second, the wind will send him soaring. He envisions himself steering through the sky and gliding to a safe landing.

Then, as quick as it came, the wind exhausts itself. Evaporates. There's no eye of the storm. The wind is just gone.

Cautious drivers step from their vehicles...

Creep to the edge of the underpass...

Witness.

Trees fallen willy-nilly across the highway. Scattered as though fractured pickup-sticks.

A voice amongst the crowd, "Is it passable...?"

There are those who say it may be best they wait for The Administration to arrive and remove the mess. For, of course, they're aware of what's happened. Now that the wind has subsided, they'll send a drone to survey the damage. Workers with saws and a mulching machine will arrive to make a path. They're infinitely efficient that way.

There are others who aren't so patient. Not enough to wait for help that may never come. At least not for a long time. Instead, they'll try to navigate the maze of fallen trees, Yeorgi among them. Even though he has shaved off his beard and his hair, he can't risk someone from The Administration recognizing him. Arresting him. Then. There.

He's come too far.
He climbs into his truck and leads the way.

***

A sudden blizzard…
In July.
But not just a skiff this time. Ankle-deep.
Wet…
Slushy…
This is how it happens nowadays.

The snow will disappear tomorrow with the next warm front. But for now, a whiteout that slows a lengthy line of vehicles navigating sluggishly through it; refugees from the fire, including Marta, "Little Robert" and Sasha, who now pilots Marta's truck.

For the past two days, Sasha answers to the name "Big Robert." It's comical that, from an infinite list of aliases he could've picked, he'd choose the same name as the kid. It must've been floating in the air waiting for his sub-conscious to reel it in as a psychic might a passing spirit.

Other than Marta and Little Robert, he's distanced himself from everybody else in the convoy. He doesn't plan to stick around much longer. It's dangerous, and the sooner he breaks away, the better. Marta is clearly a capable woman, but after she saved his life, he feels obliged to see them safely to Coal Town. Even though it's brought him dangerously near The Beige. Not only that. Just now, on the way through the town, he glimpsed one of the wanted posters The Administration has distributed. So far, it looks as though Marta is unaware of his resemblance to one rebel depicted in them. It's unlikely she's never seen the posters up close. They're everywhere. Then again, he remembers, she's just lost everything she owns. Without a doubt, she's preoccupied with finding a stable perch for her and Little Robert.

He tenses when he sees a checkpoint with a contingent of The Beige. He quells an urge to break from the convoy and bolt. But clearly, he needn't worry. Eager to get out of the storm themselves, the guards indiscriminately wave everyone past them. Sasha follows the line of evacuees. Another of The Beige directs them towards a local gymnasium where a Red Cross banner flaps in the harsh wind. A welcome sight. There'll be hot soup there, and sandwiches, and cots with warm blankets.

Along the way, dozens of those from the burnt-out town fell out of the convoy, having friends or relatives who can house them until they find their footing. But Marta and Little Robert have no one. The Administration has directed such people to Coal Town. At this minute, dozens of pre-built mini houses are wending their way to a settlement The Administration is setting up, as if overnight, on an abandoned farm outside the town. With one natural disaster after another, they've become adept at resettling people. If these refugees choose to stay, it's expected they'll either work on the surrounding farms, harvesting fruits, grains, and soybeans, or find other employment in Coal Town itself.

Even in the whiteout, Marta sees a sign in a café window: 'Server Wanted.' She says she'll make that her target. Wages from a server's job will hopefully be enough to rent a mini house. She and Little Robert were happy in their snug little apartment in the old town. But nature had other ideas. Now there's no going back.

As for Sasha, he's guarded when sharing details with Marta about where he came from and where he's going.

Yet another of The Beige materializes out of the driving snow and directs them to a nearby parking lot. As they crawl from the truck, Sasha prepares to say his goodbyes to Marta and Little Robert. It's best that he doesn't stick around, not even for a bowl of soup and a sandwich at the gymnasium. Better that he should vanish into the blizzard instead. He'll make his way to the Safehouse, which according to his neckerchief map is on the outskirts. But one of The Beige waves his arms, calling out to them through the blowing snow.

"This way…! This way…!"

In an instant, Marta picks up Little Robert and thrusts him into Sasha's arms.

"Carry the kid. He's worn-out."
"But I…"

It's too late. Marta takes the lead, striding through the snow towards the gymnasium. Biting his lip, Sasha follows nervously. As they pass the officer, Sasha shields his face behind Little Robert.

Stepping into the gymnasium and shaking off the snow, Marta takes the lead again and approaches a check-in table.

A perfunctory guard barely looks up at her.

"How many?"

"Three."

"Names…?"

Tensing, Sasha pulls Little Robert's face closer to his.

Unphased, Marta responds.

"Marta O'Hara, Little Robert and Big Robert."

The guard looks towards the tall man, his face partially obscured as he cuddles the shivering little boy. His scowl melts into a sympathetic smile as he types into a computer…

"Marta O'Hara, Robert O'Hara and Robert Junior."

He passes Marta three numbered cards.

"The numbers match the cots you're assigned. There's hot soup. The poor kid needs it."

Together, they enter the gymnasium. It teems with others from the convoy. It's as though Sasha has entered a snake pit. The Beige are everywhere, directing people. The way things are going, he fears they might end up in the centre of the overflowing room. He might as well carry a sign declaring, "Here I am. Come and get me!" But he's relieved to discover that the numbered cards correspond to cots set up in one corner.

He lays drowsy Little Robert gently onto one of them, then sits opposite with his back to the crowd as Marta draws a blanket over the boy. Then she walks away. Glancing back over her shoulder, she calls out to Sasha…

"Wait here, Love. I'll get food."

Sasha's brow furrows. "Love…?" He tucks the blanket up under Little Robert's chin.

Out of nowhere, a man's deep voice sounds behind him.

"Got everything you need…?"

Stiffening, Sasha stays turned away from the man, hoping his own voice won't betray his fear.

"Yes, thanks. Just making sure my little boy here gets warm."

Time slows. It feels as though a hammer will soon fall.

The deep voice again…

"Well, you're safe now. There's food, you know."

"Yes… yes, my… Marta's getting it."

As the man moves away, Sasha glimpses a beige uniform.

He stays with his back to the crowd as long minutes pass. Finally, Marta returns carrying a tray of food. Little Robert sits up wearily as she passes him a sandwich. She hands another to Sasha. She takes up a bowl of steaming soup and sits next to him on the cot. He turns to look at her.

"You know…don't you?"

Marta slurps a spoonful of the hot soup.

"Recognized you the minute you washed the soot off your face."

***

The punishing heat returns.

Within hours, the snow melts into a muddy slurry. It seeps into Jack's and Henry's shoes as they scramble into bushes to avoid an oncoming train.

They had sheltered in the old barn for two nights after the rainstorm became a blizzard. Once the sun returned, Henry took out a small, but heavy, box wrapped in brown paper. Inside it, he said, was Yelena's ashes. Astounded that they had found a field of wildflowers—the kind Yelena dreamed of and made her last wish—they scattered the ashes amongst the blooms, springing unrelenting through the melting snow.

Later, after checking the neckerchief map, they saw a rail line running alongside the farm leading directly to Coal Town, where the Safehouse is. It's safer to follow the track than walk the highway where someone might see them.

They've been slogging since sunrise, dodging in and out of the bush each time whooshing trains pass. They've neared the town. If they can keep a steady pace, they'll arrive just after dark. With any luck, they can easily check out the Safehouse. Henry says there'll be telltale signs of whether it's okay to approach. They can replenish provisions there and find help to recharge the MINI Cooper. They're eager to get back on the road as soon as possible.

But for now, they watch as flatbed after flatbed rolls past them, each carrying a mini house. The train is a hundred cars long and takes minutes to pass, finally disappearing around a bend. They step out of the bush and back up onto the track, where Jack scrapes a sticky clod of mud from the sole of his shoe.

"Looks like the Administration is setting up a settlement somewhere."

Sitting on a rail, Henry wrings water from his socks.

"Trying to keep one step ahead of nature, I guess."

Pulling themselves together, they shoulder their knapsacks and continue along the track, with Jack taking the lead.

Silent...

Lost in his own thoughts.

As they walk, day dissolves into dusk. Jack takes in the trees lining the track. Bowing under snow, they have dripped throughout the afternoon as clumps slide from their branches in the rising heat, plopping onto the ground...

Turning to slush...

Liquifying...

Swallowed up by the mossy earth or forming rivulets that flow beside the track...

It happens fast.

"Henry...?"

"Yes, Jack...."

"I think we're too late."

"What do you mean?"

"To keep living...."

He stops and turns to face Henry.

"If The Administration doesn't get us, the earth might."

Henry gives him a knowing smile. The kind he always does when Jack becomes wistful.

"You've been quiet too long. I just knew you were overthinking things."

"I do that, don't I."

Henry lays a hand on his shoulder.

"It's true, my love. This planet doesn't give a shit. It'll continue to exist long after it wipes us out. There are other rocks floating in the universe where there's no discernible us. And there can't be because the kinds of elements needed to sustain us just don't exist there. But still that rock exists... spinning... floating. No one controlling it; shaping it; bending it to his will the way we try to with this place; this earth. The elements we need for survival, that we bend to our will, unravel; they're falling dominoes. Turning against us. Faster than any of us ever wants to believe."

He gazes at the far horizon.

"We've fucked things up, Jack. And I, too, fear that we might be too late and will fall the same as those dominos."

He strokes the back of his hand along Jack's cheek.

"But I refuse to die on The Administration's schedule. I'll let nature take its revenge."

Jack takes in those eyes. Those pale blue eyes. Startling, even in the dimming light.

Henry leans into him.

You must remember what I've always told you, Jack. "The answer to the question, 'To be, or not to be?' is *always* 'To be....'"

"And so, to The Haven. Is that it?"

"It exists, my love. And it's magnificent. If we can just stay alive, you and me together, I promise I'll get us there, come flood or inferno."

"I've missed you, Henry."

"Of course you have. I'm terrific."

Jack laughs aloud.

"Oh, my god, the ego!"

Henry laughs along with him as they pick up the pace, trekking towards the distant lights of Coal Town, now twinkling in the twilight.

Nearer and nearer.

By the time they arrive, it's dark.

From a fringe of forest surrounding the town, they watch as a line of administration vans pulls into a full parking lot near a school. Jack points to the gymnasium and a flapping flag with the Red Cross symbol.

"Looks as though people are on the move."

"Climate refugees, maybe...."

"They're bound for those mini houses we

saw on the train."

They watch as men in beige uniforms haul cardboard food boxes into the gymnasium. Henry cringes.

"This is frightening. There's an awful lot of The Beige here."

"The Safehouse is on the other side of town, isn't it?"

"We can't walk the main street. We'll have to stick to the trees."

They spend the next hour circumnavigating the small town, working their way to the other side. It's difficult in the dark.

Low-hanging branches slap at them…

Vines entangle them…

The brambles scratch.

Finally, they arrive at a deserted street on the outskirts where they find the house they're looking for. It's a ramshackle fifty meters from the woods, its yard overgrown with weeds. A lamp glows in the window behind a faded floral-print curtain. Henry points to tin numbers nailed above the door, barely visible in a dim porch light.

"Look. Number 939."

"You think it's safe?"

"Check out the pot of geraniums on the porch."

"What of it?"

"It's placed on the righthand side of the step. That means it's safe."

But no sooner has he spoken the words than

the door opens, and a boney middle-aged woman steps onto the porch. She shifts the flowerpot from right to left.

Jack peers at Henry through the dark, confused.

"What's happening…?"

"She must've gotten word. Something's up."

The woman turns to re-enter the house when a van from The Administration speeds around the corner, followed by another. Jack and Henry duck behind bushes as headlights sweep across the yard. The two vehicles come to an abrupt halt outside the gate and half a dozen of The Beige climb out. The officer in charge casually approaches the woman on the porch. She is calm as he speaks to her.

"Evening Madam…."

Jack and Henry lean forward, straining to hear as the woman addresses the officer in charge.

"Officer. How can I help you?"

"We've come to search your house."

"Why should you want to do that?"

"We got word you have guests."

"You're mistaken, sir. I live alone."

The officer motions to the others, standing outside the gate. They stride up the path to the porch.

The woman steps in front of them, barring them.

"You have no right!"

The men in beige brush past her, shoving

her towards the officer in charge, who grabs her by her slender wrist.

The woman cries out in pain.

"Where's your warrant!"

Jack whispers.

"What's happening?"

Henry draws him deeper into the darkness.

Suddenly, a man crawls from a window at the side of the house. He breaks for the bush, running directly towards where Jack and Henry are hiding.

The officer in charge draws his pistol and fires. The man falls within yards of Jack and Henry.

Dead.

A bullet in his back.

The woman shrieks…

"No…!"

The men in beige come back out of the house dragging struggling people, each are elderly. The officer in charge lets go of the sobbing woman's wrist and crosses the yard to the dead man.

As he approaches, Jack's body jolts.

He recognizes Bateman.

Henry cups his hand over Jack's mouth and pulls him even deeper into the darkness.

Bateman, hearing something in the bush, peers into the blackness, straining to see. Smeared across his eyes is an odd streak of black paint, making him look as though he were a bandit, or a racoon.

From behind him, the woman cries out…

"He's my son! You shot my son."

Turning on heel, Bateman returns to the woman.

He forces her to her knees.

"No Madam. He was not your son. You live alone, remember?"

He aims his pistol and fires a bullet into her head.

CHAPTER 6

An affinity for gold spray-paints, meant to imitate gold-leaf…

Furniture in the French Provincial style…

Flocked wallpaper...

Dark green velveteen bedspread…

Drapes that match it, with swags and gold fringe like something out of *Gone with the Wind*…

Candelabra wall sconces and a chandelier over the bed with acrylic drops molded to look the same as hand cut crystal but which, over time, have become milky…

A faux-Persian carpet, machine woven…

Seated at her elaborate vanity in the master bedroom, the mayor's wife.

She examines her face in a lighted mirror. The fillers beauticians pumped into her cheeks took care of the crevices. And she's airbrushed away blotchy freckles, making her skin appear creamy and flawless. Today, it's imperative she appears flawless. She and the mayor must meet with an actual Senior, who arrives today from the capital to discuss their son and the spray-painted wanted poster.

She brushes a pinky finger over her eyebrows. They're perfect. And the salon has made her lashes look natural, even though they're unnaturally lush. It took two expensive hours for the technician to glue each strand of hair to the lids one at a time. Then another hour to do up her auburn hair, which has faded over the years. Despite that, no grey.

She draws her fingers over her throat and frowns. At forty-two, she's developed a turkey neck. She slides open the drawer of her vanity and withdraws a silk scarf from amongst a vast array. Blue and gold to add snap to the simple but becoming grey dress she's chosen. Grey. A sombre colour that says she appreciates the gravity of the circumstance. But not funereal. God forbids! She must not convey any wrong signals. She arranges the scarf to camouflage her throat.

Now, for scent. Something young and fresh. No. She'd better not. The Senior might have an allergy. The last thing she needs today is to sting The Senior's eyes or make him sneeze. No, no, no.

She rises from her vanity and steps up to a nearby full-length mirror, taking in the entire silhouette.

Yes. Perfect.

The mayor slouches into the bedroom and exhales a heavy sigh. He's chosen a red tie to go with his navy-blue suit.

His wife scans him from head to foot.

"Oh, lovebug. I thought you were going with the grey."

"I changed my mind."

His wife harrumphs.

"Well, at least switch your tie to the gold stripe, so we coordinate."

The mayor salutes and marches to the closet, where he slips off the red tie. He drapes it on a rack, then selects a gold stripe.

The mayor's wife takes her grandmother's diamond brooch from a jewel box and holds it up to her dress.

"Too much flash for the afternoon…?" Then, answering her own question. "Yes, too much."

She places the brooch back in the box.

The mayor fidgets with his necktie.

"I'm not sure what worries you more. Our son, or the way we're dressed."

"They're the same thing, lovebug. Understand that. We must appear humble, but worthy of due respect."

"You seem to think we're more important than we are."

"You're the mayor!"

"Of Coal Town…."

His wife patters across the room to him and takes command of the necktie, looping it into a perfect double Windsor.

"Even if it's only Coal Town, being mayor means something. And a town that's growing, what with the new settlement. Remind The Senior of that."

She smooths the necktie and tucks it into the mayor's jacket.

"We're as good as any Senior from the capital."

***

Alistair Goodwin watches as an enormous crane swings the last of the mini houses into place. It's one of a hundred that arrived by train from a factory in the middle of the country, creating an entire subdivision overnight. Ready for the refugee families to occupy. Former shipping containers repurposed into streamlined self-contained components laid out across the farmer's field in a precise grid; singles or joined in twos or threes, depending on the size of the family. It's incredibly efficient.

Work crews installing pylons and the crane making its way back and forth across the field have crushed the wildflowers that once grew there. But, being wildflowers, with luck and the strength of nature, they may spring up again.

Alistair turns his attention to the old barn. The crew sent to raze it to prepare for the settlement, discovered an abandoned MINI Cooper there. It looked as if the vehicle hadn't been in the barn long. Suspicion arose when they couldn't prove ownership, and further investigation showed that the plate number is false. Alistair dug into the data and produced a partial image of a similar MINI Cooper. A camera had captured it at the site of a former rebel house, which The Administration had bulldozed. Even though only three numbers on the plate were visible in the photo, they matched numbers belonging to the MINI Cooper found in the barn. Alistair suspects the vehicle connects to either the elderly people which Bateman captured in Coal Town or the Amphorium bombers. He instructed the demolition crew to leave the car where it lay. A team is assembling to do a thorough examination.

Alistair swings open the barn doors and peers in.

The MINI Cooper, abandoned…

Footprints in the dust…

Fingerprints on surfaces…

Possible DNA.

First clues to the whereabouts of one or more of the Amphorium bombers.

***

A windowless room…

Spartan…

Silent…

Walls painted a murky grayish green…

Dim overhead lighting…

A wooden table and chairs…

Seated alone, the mayor's son.

He looks at a large two-way mirror built into one wall. He senses mysterious people watching him from a darkened room on the other side. Defiant, he raises his middle finger at the mirror then laughs aloud, realizing he's not only flipped-the-bird to the observers, but to his own reflection. He wonders who he's angrier at, the authorities for capturing him, or himself, because this time he didn't escape. No matter. He'll be out of this dingy room soon enough. Once his father works his magic; wields power. Being the son of the mayor serves him well.

Always.

Minutes later, a door swings open and Alistair Goodwin strides into the room. He takes a seat opposite the boy.

Wordless...

Unblinking...

Waiting.

Crossing his arms over his stomach, Goodwin leans back in his chair. The Administration must decide; make a choice. He peers into the boy's eyes. Indeed, past them and into his soul, looking for something that might provide the answer.

The boy waits too. Wordless. He understands the game well. In circumstances such as these, whoever speaks first loses. Still, Goodwin is a patient man.

He never expected to find himself in a place such as Coal Town. But recent incidents have transformed the place into a hotbed. First, there was the embarrassing RV episode outside town. The Administration expected to capture the Amphorium bombers live on camera. Instead, they terrorized an innocent family in front of the entire nation. Then a fire destroyed a village in the north, forcing the resettlement of climate refugees to mini houses nearby. The Senior jumped on the opportunity to visit the settlement to bring needed positive publicity to The Administration. But, just after announcing his visit, two new incidents occurred in Coal Town, which threaten to upend it. Both involving Bateman.

Not only did he kill—or slaughter, depending on your point of view—a mother and her son at a so-called rebel house, there's an assault on him by this boy; the mayor's son—who vandalized a poster. An incident which should've needed only a mild reprimand has spiralled out of control and become a political nightmare.

And the nation is watching.

Either there's proof of a two-tiered hierarchy, where those with a connection within The Administration act with impunity and walk away. Or the law of Each-one-for-Everyone applies, and they "Eveningsong" an enemy of the people, the same as those at the rebel house were. The question is: Is the boy an enemy of the people or just a boy?

If they Eveningsong the mayor's son, The Administration satisfies those who believe in the law of Each-one-for-Everyone. But infusing the boy for such a minor infraction might incite

The Fringe to more violent acts. Then again, more serious infractions could happen if The Administration doesn't circumvent the minor ones.

Goodwin wishes life were simpler.

Fifteen minutes pass and not a word spoken as the boy and Goodwin sit staring at one another. Still, Goodwin is much better at the game. His unwavering gaze at the boy is blank. Empty. Whereas the boy's return gaze betrays a thousand insights for Goodwin: first, defiance. Then anger, bewilderment, fear, resolve and, at last, submission.

Leaning forward, the boy speaks.

"What do you want me to say? I'm a naughty boy…? I didn't mean to break the law…? I'll never do it again…? What…."

Goodwin stays silent. Entwining his fingers, he leans into the boy, ready to listen. Startled, the boy's eyes widen, and he sits back.

"I don't have to say another word, you know. My dad will be here soon. He's the mayor of this shit hole. Did you know that? The *may*or."

He's surprised when Goodwin doesn't react to the implication: the sudden realization that this circumstance is unlike any other he's met for any of his earlier transgressions. His father always outranks everyone in the room when untangling messes. This time Goodwin trumps a mayor.

So, minimize.

"It was just a poster, for Pete's sake. A piece

of paper on a wall. What's the big deal?"

He looks at Goodwin, waiting for a response. There is none.

"Yeah, I know it was The Group-of-Five. Do you think that makes me one of them? You think I wanna blow up the world...?"

He chuckles.

Goodwin is a stone.

Justify.

"They have a right to their anger, you know. You're killing people before their time. Sure, it's the law of Each-one-for-Everyone. But it's fucked. It's an unjust law, past its time. The earth's healing. We don't need that law anymore...."

Goodwin leans back in his chair, knowing that what comes next from the boy is an accusation.

"It's nothing but murder, you know. You and your kind are nothing but murderers! I have a right to protest, don't I...? Don't I? We should wipe your kind off the face of the earth."

In for a penny.

"You're damn right I'm one of them. I revere The Group-of-Five for what they've done. I hope they do more...."

Goodwin has let it go too far. He opens his mouth to speak, but the boy continues, tears now flooding his eyes.

"When I get free, I'll blow you all up...!"

Goodwin's face betrays emotion for the first time. A steely glare. Others, including The Senior behind the mirror, are recording everything. The boy's words are now a permanent record.

The boy opens his mouth to speak again. But Goodwin shocks him, to bring him back to his senses, back into the world. He scrapes his chair loudly across the floor and stands.

With that, he strides out of the room, leaving the tearful boy alone to ponder.

***

A living room overdressed...

Bric-à-brac on every single surface...

A silver-plated tea and coffee service...

Fine porcelain cups and saucers...

A cut crystal vase with a cheerful posy...

The mayor and his wife sit together in silence, awaiting The Senior.

He's late.

Worry hangs in the air. Things may have gone too far with their son this time.

The mayor is uncertain whether his wife understands the danger. To her, the black spray-paint was only a boy's faux pas, a betrayal of social niceties. But the mayor knows The Senior's eyes will tell. They'll be judge and jury. If he looks into the eyes of the mayor and his wife when they greet, then he'll save their son. If he avoids them, then the boy doesn't stand a chance.

The mayor's wife suggested they meet with The Senior at their home to discuss the boy, instead of in a stuffy office at Townhall.

It makes the occasion more intimate. More personal. She suggested they lay out tea, coffee, light sandwiches, and pastries. It's hospitable and makes everything less official; just friends meeting for a casual chat as if over a game of whist.

The mayor looks at his wife, sitting now, erect in a straight-backed chair, her legs crossed at the ankles. She adjusts her silk scarf, then picks up a cup and saucer, holding it with the utmost delicacy. Lost in thought, she sips the steaming tea. To the mayor's dismay, she spent a large part of her food budget on the genuine stuff: expensive imported black tea. And the coffee too. Anything to toady up to The Senior.

"Lovebug…is The Senior a coffee man, or a tea man…?"

The mayor drifts out of his own deep contemplation.

"Hmm…?"

"The Senior. Does he drink tea or coffee?"

"Not sure."

The mayor's wife drifts back into her own thoughts.

"I hope it will be tea…."

After twenty years together, the mayor knows his wife applies significance to things such as a preference for tea or coffee. She's gotten it into her mind that a man who favours tea is more civil than one who drinks coffee; is less brusque, with more heart; has more compassion. The mayor doesn't know why she believes these notions. It's the sort of idea her lady's group gives credence; the appropriateness of a diamond brooch in the afternoon, or the implications of being a mayor's wife as opposed to the wife of a clerk.

She takes another sip.

"The Senior's wife... Sherrie? No. Cherise. That's right, Cherise."

Her brow crinkles as she draws more of The Senior's details from her memory.

"And the children. Prunella and Rosie. Is that correct...?"

"I think so, yes."

"It's important to get these things right, you know."

She's been a potent ally during the mayor's political rise; from school trustee to a chair in town counsel, then to the leader of the entire town.

Even in a small municipality, such as Coal Town, prominent families exist. The mayor's wife knows who they are and all their pertinent details: names, birthdays, noteworthy events in their lives. Her memory for such minutiae is eidetic. Facts rise from the file cabinet that is her mind and float in the air as images above the heads of people she meets: name–Harvey Bergen, wife–Emily Bergen, children... etcetera. The smallest detail picked up along the way. Prefers red wine to white—allergic to shrimp. All noted in each person's individual mental file for immediate retrieval whenever necessary. Without doubt, with her at his side, the mayor will one day rise to a senior position in The Administration.

Unless their wayward son sideswipes the plan.

The mayor's wife sets her teacup on the table and wanders to the window. Pensive, she gazes out through a lacy curtain to the street, mumbling as if to herself alone.

"I'd remember if ever I saw The Senior choose coffee over tea...."

As the mayor watches his wife, he knows that she's planning her approach. When greeting The Senior, she'll draw on the proper details. In her charming way, she'll revere The Senior for his power and, without insult, note that the mayor and his family are of the same class as he. They're worthy of consideration beyond the norm.

Their son is worthy beyond the norm.

It's true the boy has been a handful since an early age. The mayor wonders if they've done him any favours, bending to his will once too often. At every opportunity, the mayor's wife tells their son he's special. Even though his IQ tests average, and he has no outstanding talent. After years of piano lessons, he's only competent. And as an athlete, he's only mediocre. Truth-be-told, he's run-of-the-mill. The mayor believes the boy could live a happy life if his mother didn't press him to be more than he is. And he wonders if their son acts out because deep inside, he knows he's not superior and is struggling to prove it. Worse still, he may have taken in what his mother told him throughout his life and now believes his superiority and that he can get away with whatever he wants.

The mayor admits—at least to himself—his part in it. He's not only given the boy everything he needs, but everything he wants. Such as the expensive new car after high school graduation which, not a week later, he rolled into a ditch and destroyed while on a drunken joyride with friends. It's lucky he didn't kill anyone, although one boy sustained crippling lifelong injuries. The mayor wrote a large check to make it go away. The check was much less than it could've been, because the mayor knew that the father of the disabled boy aspired to first-floor quarters in a nicer house. And he implied he had the pull to get it for him.

For a while now, he suspected his son had taken to tagging public property with black spray-paint; vandalism, which the mayor had cleaned up under the guise of the 'Civic Pride Program,' which the town budget funds. The defacement of the poster confirmed the mayor's suspicion. But it was just that, and only that. Straightforward defacement of property. It had nothing to do with any sympathy for The Group-of-Five. Even though the boy is of a political family, it was not a political act. It was a boy being a boy. The Senior must understand that.

The mayor's wife is still at the window, gazing out, musing.

"Coffee or tea. Either way, we'll rise to the

challenge...."

She stiffens as through the lacy curtain she sees a black electric glide up in front of the house. The Senior steps out and makes his way up the walk....

***

Bateman swipes his hand across a steamy bathroom mirror and examines his reflection. Try as he may, he cannot scrub away the band of black paint across his face. The only thing to do is wait for the remnants to flake off with dead skin cells. In the meantime, he endures the taunts of his fellow officers. Worse still, the taunts of trainees he considers inferior. Ginni, in her course and abrupt way, has taken to calling him 'Bandit.' At least Lila Wong does her best to hide her amusement, biting a lip whenever she looks his way. Still, he can't help wondering if he's lost her respect as well.

But it's not just the paint.

Ever since the killings at the rebel house, his fellow Beige treat him differently. The vast majority drew a thin line at once and circled the wagons. But not everyone. Lila, for instance. He doesn't know where she stands. She's been circumspect with her comments.

Damn it, he was just doing his job.

He splashes icy water onto his face, running wet fingers through his hair. Yes, it turns out that the escaping man he shot was the woman's son. And yes, he killed a rebel woman who was not at the time resisting—although that's not the story he and his fellow Beige detailed in their incident reports. But it's the same outcome. The woman and her son were traitors to the people. Eveningsong was their fate, but with infusion instead of a bullet. He just saved the state the price of an infusion ceremony. Even though he didn't follow procedure to the letter, hadn't he sent a simple message to discourage rebel houses in the future?

Yes, damn it, he did his job.

Today, one of two things will happen. The Senior will either put him on administrative leave or charge him with murder. There was a time when he had confidence in The Administration; of no charges against him. But sentiment towards The Beige has changed. The populace has lost confidence. They question The Beige and their actions and even call for complete abolition. The thought sparks Bateman to speak aloud to his own image in the mirror: "Oh, yeah? When someone breaks into your house, who you gonna call…?"

He pulls back. Talking to himself in the mirror is not a healthy sign.

Later, he stands before the same mirror dressed in his smart uniform. Not a crease, buttons polished. He feels the old confidence flow back into his body. Yes, there he is. Cock of the walk. He grabs his crotch and squeezes: "Cock and balls, man. Cock and balls…"

He does not doubt The Senior will take his side over the rebels. And over a dumbass kid. Even if he is the mayor's son. Surely.

***

The tick of a grandfather clock…

Lemon-scented wood polish infuses the room.

As he sips, The Senior sniffs the paper-thin slice of lemon floating atop the steaming pekoe. He would have preferred to savour real coffee. But for an inexplicable reason, the mayor's polite wife had urged forward the silver-plated teapot when she asked, "Coffee or tea, Senior…?" She smiled, as if relieved when he relented and opted for tea, assuring him that its authentic black and not a weak herbal.

He scans the room. The bric-à-brac feels oppressive: a dozen or more Dresden dolls in a cabinet, porcelain flowers in a glass dome, and elaborate silver spoons latched into an oak plaque in the shape of a world map, inherited from a well-travelled maiden aunt who carried back a souvenir teaspoon from each stop along her way. Copies of famous paintings hang here and there in gilded frames. An old-world Victorian parlour. He wonders if each room in the house is the same as this one. Overdone.

The mayor's wife has left open a window to let in a feeble sultry breeze, and everything is spit polished. Still, an aura of antique dust drifts throughout the room. Ghosts of former owners of the bric-à-brac move here and there in silence. They pass through walls and climb the stair.

The Senior suspects everything comes from the wife's side of the family and is significant to her; fragments of her long since faded heritage. He glimpses the mayor's profile, reflected in a gilded mirror hanging next to a certified copy of Monet's water lilies, suspecting he doesn't care for any of it. It's important to his wife, and that's what matters.

Her voice draws The Senior out of his dusty lemon-scented ghost thoughts...

"He's just a boy. They're naïve at that age, aren't they? Another sandwich, Senior…?"

"Hmm…?"

The mayor's wife lifts a plate stacked with pastries.

"Or a cookie…?"

The Senior takes in an antique butter churn near the fireplace.

"No thanks. You've stuffed me." He pats his stomach.

The mayor's wife smiles proudly as she sets the plate on the table.

"As I was saying, he's always been… impetuous."

She looks towards her husband.

"Don't you agree, dear? Impetuous…?"

The mayor's eyes shift from The Senior to his wife. He nods. Then his eyes shift back to The Senior as his wife continues.

"One tries to give everything they need as they grow. Instruct them. Make them decent people. But they're young. Inexperienced. They can't, for their life, see what's beyond their actions. Don't you agree Senior…?"

The Senior takes in a cheap ceramic rooster on a shelf, shoddier than the other souvenirs. Odd and out of place.

The mayor's wife invades his thoughts again.

"Your children, Senior. Rosie and Prunella, I believe…."

"Yes."

"Twins, I remember. Five now…?"

"Six."

"Six! Growing fast. Before you know it, they'll be teens. And impetuous, the same as our boy…."

She notices The Senior's face darken.

"That's not to say it's not serious. It is. It wasn't just any poster, was it? We understand the significance. Don't we, dear?"

Attempting to catch The Senior's eye, the mayor speaks.

"He's a boy, Senior. Just a boy."

The Senior sets his cup on the table. It's an eternity to the mayor and his wife as he sits in quiet contemplation. At last, he speaks.

"I'm sure…."

He stands, brushing off crumbs from his pants, smoothing out wrinkles from sitting so long.

"I have much to consider. But I must go now. I must check out the new settlement."

The mayor's wife springs to her feet and holds out her hand to him.

"Should my husband accompany you? The mayor could help you navigate any press that might be there."

"Unnecessary. But thank you."

He crosses the room towards the door with the mayor and his wife trailing after him.

The mayor again, "He's just a boy, Senior. A boy...."

The mayor and his wife stand on the porch and watch as The Senior makes his way along the walk, climbs into his electric, and drives away.

The mayor's wife waves after him. Then, to her husband...

"'Much to consider....' What do you think he meant...?"

She turns to the mayor, who looks ashen as he watches The Senior's car disappear around a corner.

During their entire meeting, The Senior had taken in the bric-à-brac, the cookies on the tray, the tea and even the ceramic rooster; a cheap trinket their son had won at a carnival when he was ten years old and, with great pride, presented to his mother.

But not once, even as he drove away, had The Senior looked directly into the eyes of the mayor.

Nor his wife.

CHAPTER 7

Choking tar...

Grinding metal...

Wheels screech as the train rounds a wide arc. Soon it will penetrate the prairies. There will be no more slow curves, just straight rails for miles and miles and miles.

Trembling, Jack presses deeper into Henry's chest. It's not the dank air that makes him shiver. But rage...

Fear...

Grief.

The shock of seeing Bateman again. The man who had held a gun to his head and made him choose only William, or William *and* him. Then seeing him hold a gun to the old woman's head and this time pull the trigger. Huddling with Henry on a flatbed rail car in the grey early morning light, with the acrid smell of tar and the grinding wheels ringing in his ears, he wishes Bateman dead.

A cruel death.

His vehemence shocks him, his need for

vengeance. Bateman's eyes for William's eyes. Bateman's teeth for those of the old woman. Old Testament justice.

Sensing Jack's rage, Henry pulls him closer, radiating body heat into him. Wanting to soothe him, quell him although he too is full of rage.

After seeing the slaughter, they had fled back through the forest: vines entangling, brambles tearing at their skin, roots tripping. If Bateman had sensed their presence in the wood, seeing his crime, he never followed or sent anyone to pursue them. And so, Jack and Henry had arrived back at the railway track in time to hop a westbound freight train. Pressed against the floor of a boxcar in the dimness, they'd rolled through the town unnoticed. Hopping from train to train for two days and evading security, according to Henry's neckerchief map, the rail line will soon pass through another town with a Safehouse. If it's there, still. If The Beige hasn't raided it.

Morning light is rising, and the flattening landscape poses a threat. Forests are thinning as the train rolls toward open prairie. More often now, the rail line nears the transcontinental highway, following parallel. Henry and Jack huddle at the heel of a flatbed, but it will be obvious to passing motorists that two men are riding the rails as if they are depression-era vagabonds. And if a drone passes; if facial recognition processes them, they're done. They can only hope the train arrives in the next town before the sun reaches its peak and before traffic on the highway increases.

They've eaten little in the past two days and had little to drink. When the heat rises on the open prairie, their throats will parch. The notion that they're nearing a Safehouse is the only thing that keeps them going. That, and Henry's constant reassurance that The Haven exists. It's still far, far away. But it's real.

Henry calls out over the clatter of the train.

"When we get to the Safehouse, look for a signal."

Jack cocks a ringing ear to take in the words.

"The same as the flowerpot at the last place, you mean."

"Or maybe something red or green."

Jack looks back at him, perplexed.

"Green means safe. Red means stay away...."

Jack laughs. It's something out of a cheap novel describing the French Resistance.

As the train journeys away from the forests and then further away from rocky, rolling hills, it rumbles into fresh territory, picking up speed. It's as though God took a giant rolling pin to the landscape, making it as flat as a tabletop. Having only flown over it, and never having experienced it at eye level, it's astounding to Jack.

But not Henry.

Although he hasn't told Jack, he came this way a year ago, while he and Jack were no longer together. Only Henry wasn't riding the rails then.

Instead, he was driving the highway running parallel, together with Yelena.

Now they gaze out over the expanse. The unobstructed panorama is so vast, they can see two weather systems at the same time. Above them, and for miles, blue sky, and sun. But in the distant northwest, an isolated cloud with a flash of lightning inside it, and with sheets of pelting rain from its underside. And straight ahead, a dark jagged line on the horizon. Buildings.

Jack points. "Is that the town…?"

Henry holds a hand up to shade his eyes, squinting. "I think so."

"Maybe we should hop off the train before we get too close."

"No. Not yet. The flatlands are deceptive. That town's further away than it looks. We'll wait for the train to slow."

Henry's right. It's a long time before they arrive near the outskirts of the town and sense the train's decreasing speed.

The sun sears their skin.

Gathering up their knapsacks, they take the leap, landing and rolling onto the hard-packed ground. The shock of it ricochets throughout their bodies.

Stumbling to his feet, Henry moans, "Christ, it's hard getting old…."

They watch as the train rumbles toward the distant town, becoming a black dot, disappearing. They scan the landscape. It's remarkable to think that the rail bed is the highest point in this desolate place. There are wheat fields stretching as far as they can see. But they're under-watered, roasting in the sun. Stunted.

Jack and Henry don't have to walk far before Henry points to a house, standing isolated in a field...

Alone...

A wallflower at a barn dance.

By chance, luck is with them. Strung out on a clothesline, drying in the searing heat are bright white bedsheets and a lone shirt, brilliant green.

From inside the house, a man watches through a slit in the window curtains as the two strangers make their way across a yellowed, brittle lawn to the front porch. He waves his hand, shewing away someone behind him. A bedroom door shuts quietly.

From outside, Jack and Henry sense that someone watches them. With trepidation, they approach, sensing a wary person inside the house. As wary as they are themselves. They've taken every precaution. But now they'll find out if The Beige has set a trap; if they've deciphered the red and green and have compromised the Safehouse. Exhausted and starving in this desolate landscape, they have no choice but to take a chance.

They step onto the porch and knock.

The door swings open at once, revealing a large, muscular man; his complexion, dark and ruddy, his hands rough-skinned, he's someone who works the land. He takes in Jack and Henry, analyzing, waiting for them to speak.

Then, his gruff voice: "Well...?"

Henry is ready with a story.

"Sorry to intrude, but... but our vehicle gave out on the highway. We wonder if you can spare a glass of water before we walk the rest of the way into town."

The farmer gazes toward the road, squinting into the distance.

"You must've walked miles. I don't see no car."

"Yes. Miles...."

"In this heat...?"

With his mouth curling into a grin, he swings wide the door.

"Come in Henry Chagall and Jack Parnell...."

Hearing their names from this stranger, Jack and Henry bolt off the porch to the yard.

The farmer calls after them. "No, no, wait. You're safe...!"

Jack and Henry look back at him, hesitant. Holding up his hand, the farmer speaks again, chuckling. "Didn't mean to frighten you."

Still distrustful, Jack exhales. "You know who we are, then...."

From somewhere behind the farmer, a woman's voice.

"Of course, he knows. Your faces are everywhere."

The farmer steps aside, revealing Elizabeth.

***

Yeorgi has spent the night in the back of his truck, swatting away mosquitoes between bouts of fitful sleep and frightening dreams. He fights his way out of a tangled, sweaty sleeping bag. His body creaks as he stretches this way and that, working out a crick in his neck. Unzipping his pants, he fires a steaming, steady stream over the edge of the truck bed into the dust.

The swelling in his knee and ankle has not subsided. He wonders if he might have cracked something when he leaped from Katarina's window. An icepack might help if he can make it to a charging station or the next Safehouse.

Two days ago, he led a convoy through the broken pickup-sticks which, for a couple hundred years, had existed as a forest before the downburst. Sometimes the drivers had to work together to heave-ho a fallen tree from the highway.

Oh, the pain in his leg. But they must not see. They must not know.

Once free of the ruin, he pulled ahead, creating a distance between him and the others. Seeing them split off and go their own way, he felt relief. He didn't want to risk anyone finding him out. Then again, they too may be fugitives on the run. Why else risk a perilous journey through a devastated forest?

He drove until exhaustion, then discovered a grove of trees off the highway in which to conceal himself and his truck.

Now, standing there in the morning light, and among the twitter of birds, he feels a rumble in his empty stomach. Food has run low. He must either find a Safehouse or risk stopping at a public charging station where he can fill up on a veggie burger and gather up supplies. It's not that he'd underestimated what he might need while fleeing. It's important to travel light. If The Beige stop him, he doesn't want an over abundance of stores to be his giveaway. Then again, if he can't avoid The Beige, too many supplies will be the least of his worries.

But he has a contingency plan.

He flips aside a tarpaulin, revealing a red metal toolbox, thinking, *God help me if it comes to that.*

There, in the dawn, feeling the cool morning dew on his skin, he reflects on the choices that brought him to this exact time, this place. Running to save his life.

Rebellious choices.

If he lives, it'll be an act of defiance. If he dies, God grant him a day such as this...

And a place such as this...

A dawn with dew on his skin, and the smell of birch, poplar, and evergreen.

His love for Trinket wells up in him. And his hatred for Katarina. His longing for the father who walked out. The anger that tilted him toward learning how to build a bomb; to want to blow up the entire world. End the universe. The irony sinking in that he flees to defy those who end lives on their terms, when he himself has it in his power to end their lives using a detonator tucked in his shirt pocket; for the right to die on his terms, or a natural end: today, tomorrow, or well past sixty. Who are they to tell him? These angry thoughts and more swirling in his aching head. And the pain in his leg. Oh, the pain in his leg, getting worse.

Then he sees it...

A distant drone.

Right now, only a black dot floating above the highway as it tracks a parade of traffic coming his way—more climate refugees. Sometimes the drone dips as if to peer into car windows at the occupants; scanning them; feeding information into big data.

Leaping to the ground, Yeorgi scrambles under the truck bed, intense pain shooting up his injured leg.

He waits. The drone may pass.

He hears the high-pitched whir of propellers, the robotic eye scanning back and forth, back, and forth...

Nearer still.

The drone hovers beside the grove like a wasp over carrion.

It has glimpsed something. A shadow in the grove. The drone's eye zooms in, taking in the dark shape. Shooting upwards, it hangs over the trees, its camera lens recording an abandoned black truck. Then the drone lowers into the trees to peer into windows; swaying branches endangering its propellers.

It shoots upwards and whirs to the other side of the grove, lowering again, taking in everything.

Underneath the truck, Yeorgi stiffens.

He's thankful the drone can go no lower because the blowing weeds edging the grove are tall. They pose a threat.

The eye swivels this way and that, scanning the full length of the truck.

From its iris, a red flash.

The urge to scramble from beneath the truck and bolt engulfs Yeorgi, or even to attack the drone. Still, he lays there.

Rigid...

Waiting.

At last, the drone shoots up and over the trees to the highway. A buzzing insect, it zips away as fast as it came.

Only then does Yeorgi realize he has held his breath throughout the ordeal. Feeling faint, he gulps the air.

Crawling from his hiding place covered in dust, he scrambles into the truck. Then, cramming it into gear, he speeds along the highway, passing the onslaught of refugee vehicles heading in the opposite direction.

***

Sasha, at the wheel of Marta's vehicle, does a double take. Had his eyes deceived him, or was that Yeorgi in the black truck speeding past them? It looked the same as the one Sasha remembers Yeorgi driving the night of the bombing. But how could that be? They'd each driven away in different directions. Then again, he himself did not expect to be in this part of the country. Fate and angry nature had forced him here. It could be the same with Yeorgi. But if he's heading into Coal Town, he'll face an unfriendly welcome. There's rising resentment among the locals around climate refugees. They want them out. And not just to a new subdivision at an abandoned farm on the outskirts.

The way the locals see it, the refugees will diminish scant resources: water, grains, fruits, and vegetables. Let them settle anywhere but Coal Town.

As Sasha, Marta, Little Robert and one hundred others left the village for the new settlement, they faced angry glares from locals lining the main street. One or two flipped them the bird as if saying, "*Go back to where you came from.*"

But they can't go back.

When bewildered Little Robert, now seated between Sasha and his mother, asked why the people did that, Marta could only respond that they're afraid. Even more confused, Little Robert wondered why people should fear a six-year-old.

To him, everything is personal.

As they drive through the countryside, Sasha looks over the cornfields. With little rain, the crops are undersized and shrivelled. No wonder the Coal Towners react the way they do.

Within minutes, Sasha, Marta, and Little Robert arrive at the new subdivision. What The Administration has supplied is, at most, utilitarian. They have laid out dozens of repurposed metal shipping containers in a precise grid, with a door and the smallest of windows cut into each one; each container-home ten feet wide by forty feet long, with a drab grey exterior that is impersonal and ugly.

On the inside, more basic functionality with slender partitioned areas for sleeping. A kitchenette/dining/sitting room takes up the remaining space. Built-in furnishings are minimal, but practical. Each unit uses solar energy, with insulation against weather. Even though dreadful, Marta says she can soon make it homey. And Sasha believes it.

Once again, she had taken charge when The Administration assigned container-homes. When the man in beige, the same functionary who checked them in at the gymnasium that snowy night, had asked for papers, Marta offered hers and explained that the fire had destroyed "Big Robert's" documents.

The administrator had looked toward the man he knew as Mr. O'Hara, his back now turned to him while tending Little Robert, and accepted Marta's story.

"Of course, Mr. O'Hara must apply for replacement papers at once."

"Of course, sir."

The man in beige clarified to her in his obligatory way that, since she was the one with papers, she must sign her name on leasing documents, and so she must oversee the prompt payment of rents to The Administration.

"Of course, sir."

As a man on the run, this arrangement suits Sasha. Although he did his best to avoid everyone at the gymnasium, he worries that, even though most had sunk into their own problems, one or two may have resurfaced long enough to recognize him as one of The Group-of-Five. He doesn't plan to stay around long. Once he settles Marta and Little Robert into their new home, he'll have fulfilled his self-imposed duty.

Not having a vehicle poses a problem for him. But, remembering the black truck speeding past them on the highway, he thinks of Yeorgi. If it was his co-conspirator who was driving, Sasha plans to make his way back to Coal Town to find him. They can hit the road again together.

If he can't find Yeorgi, Sasha is uncertain what he'll do. While still at the gymnasium, he'd caught wind of the slaughter of the keeper of the Safehouse and the bulldozing, making it impossible to seek help there.

But for now, he sits watching as Little Robert explores the nooks and crannies of the shipping container, tracing his tiny fingers over surfaces and peering into the miniscule bedrooms. In one, is a single bed for a child. In the other is a double bed for the presumed "Mr. and Mrs. Robert O'Hara."

Sasha turns his gaze to Marta, who digs into the care package The Administration supplied, contemplating the meals she can make from it, and if it'll last until her first paycheck. Then, thinking of the town's bias towards refugees, she thinks of the 'Help Wanted' sign at the cafe and wonders if the owner will give her the server position. No matter. She'll survive. She always has.

Even though his feelings for Marta have developed during their struggles together, Sasha has no plan to share the double bed. As much as he senses Marta may invite it, and as much as he may want it, it's unfair. No. He'll sleep on the floor in the main room and slip out in the morning. He'll leave it to Marta to explain his sudden disappearance to Little Robert, who now explores the built-in drawers under his bed.

Sasha envisions Marta's transformation of the shipping container into something cozy and inviting. In his vision, he has scouted out and installed larger recycled windows to let in more light. He sees himself working in the cornfields and tending wild plants that spring up around their hovel. Everyone nowadays prizes whatever sprouts, be it a weed or something more useful. Even if a weed, people now understand that everything has its place in the ecology. Everything must survive for the sake of everything else.

He sees himself painting the outside of the container bright yellow, sky blue, or even orange to distinguish it from the others. And planting flowers. He contemplates how, throughout his life, he's always had ill timing. If only all of this had come to him before the bomb plot. If only they lived in his grandparent's time, or his parent's, when such a life was possible.

But no.

As much as he may want to stay and create everything he envisions for real, it's a danger to him, and to Marta and Little Robert.

So, he'll leave.

***

"Elizabeth…!"

She turns to see Jack step off the back porch of what looks like a doll's house against the vast prairie sky. He strikes out across the field to where she now stands in a sea of swaying wheat. She wants to take in one of the dramatic sunsets, renowned in big sky country. The way it's shaping up, it will not disappoint her.

Brushing his fingers over the tops of the wheat, Jack wends his way through the field, following the path Elizabeth had trampled until he arrives beside her. Minutes pass as they stand in silence, taking in streaks of red, orange, and purple forming across the expanse. In time, Jack speaks...

"Do you think any of those clouds have rain in them?"

Elizabeth purses her lips.

"Doubt it...."

More silence, although Elizabeth senses Jack's mind is a cacophony of thoughts. She saw it in his eyes, along with his surprise upon seeing her when he and Henry arrived at the Safehouse; the same young woman he had first seen at Yelena's Eveningsong. Then again, the night they fled the city after the bombing. No one introduced themselves to Jack during their ride in the escape van, and not as they each climbed into their own separate vehicles and sped away. So, now she waits for the questions she knows will come. Until then, she turns her face into the rising west wind. Was her prediction wrong? Is rain coming?

Jack snaps the head off a stem and twirls it between his fingers.

"I'm glad Henry finally introduced us, Elizabeth. He's told me so much about you."

"Has he...?"

Another silence...

Empty time.

Jack speaks again...

"Algorithms...."

Elizabeth continues her gaze at the rich sunset, a slight smile spreading, waiting for what else Jack may know. If anything, scant details.

It's clear to Jack that Elizabeth has called his bluff.

"Truth is, Henry has told me next to nothing."

"He knows next to nothing."

"I don't understand…."

Elizabeth, too, snaps the head off a stem, rubbing it between her fingers to release the grains into her palm. She curls her fingers over them.

"We also know little of Henry's details, beyond what's public record: you, William."

Hearing William's name stings Jack. But of course, his name and his story are part of big data. Anyone could suss it out.

"Why? Why don't you know more?"

"Because it's the deal we made, in case The Administration captures any of us. We'll have little to give them. They've already gathered detailed data, anyway. I know. I used to work for them."

She catches herself.

"See? Right there, I betrayed my promise. I exposed an important fact. But it's nothing Henry and the others don't already know. It's why I'm part of the group. But don't worry. I wasn't deep enough in the red to know every one of your details."

"The red…?"

Elizabeth, her face awash in golden light from the sunset, twitches into the tight-lipped smile she has perfected to suppress her sometimes loose lips.

Jack senses he'll get nothing more. He thrusts his hands into his pockets. He hates what they've had to become to survive.

Secretive…

Untrusting…

Apprehensive around anyone who asks too many questions. It fills social interaction with silences: gruff, cautious…

Fearful of betrayal.

Humanity's journey to this point was insidious. In what had been a free country, tyrannical governance arrived in dribs and drabs, a slow creep towards total loss of freedom. Jack had watched as the masses became infatuated with a regime that offered simple solutions to dire ecological problems threatening human existence. Only through mending fractures in thought, they said, and bringing together smaller factions into one big bloc, could it then survive.

But Jack remembers his history. The world has been here before, again, and again, and again. The difference being that there's no individual culture at risk. Instead, all of it. Each person, every culture, no matter their politics. When nature turns against you; when melting ice fractures mountainsides, causing them to crumble and topple upon you, it's time to act.

For Jack, it's too little too late.

From an early age, he saw what was coming. He didn't set out to be a preacher. Preaching was telling and telling isn't teaching. But his journalism hollered the gospel of preserving nature. Not for its own sake, but for the survival of freedom. Even as a child, he envisioned the tyranny that follows the destruction of a forest, the air, water. But few, especially the greedy, listened to the likes of him, believing the power lay in their hands and not nature's. Believing they had more time than they did. And so, set targets too far into the future.

Now, riverbeds dry to a trickle, oceans rise and swallow the land, mountainsides fall away and those who once loved one another with each beating breath are now suspicious and fearful.

Jack hates his cynicism. But he cannot for his life see a good end to any of it.

He takes one last look at the fading sunset.

"We're exposed out here. I think I'll go back."

He pauses, hoping that Elizabeth might reveal more.

Nothing.

He turns and wends his way back to the doll's house.

Elizabeth watches him go. She, too, feels exposed in the immense landscape. If a drone passes overhead now, she'll have no place to hide herself. Still, she'll take in the fiery sunset to its last glowing ember.

She unfurls her hand and sets free the grains she'd gathered, allowing them to float away on the mounting breeze, to seed themselves elsewhere.

She'd wanted to be more forthcoming with

Jack; to tell how she and the others had found each other; had formed what people now call The Group-of-Five; how they came to hatch their plot to bomb The Amphorium. But she'll leave such details to Henry if he wants to share them with the love of his life.

For now, she must take care of herself.

Get herself to safety.

And, most important, prove her father's suspicions about The Administration before they murdered him.

For her, bombing The Amphorium is just the beginning.

Then, with a great suddenness, a boundless roar shocks her into the present moment.

Erupting from the eastern sky, are two high-flying supersonic fighter jets. They drag behind them an ear-splitting shriek as they rocket across the sky, heading west into the fading light.

CHAPTER 8

Amber liquid in a crystal tumbler...

Scotch, neat...

The bottle, out of its hiding place in a bottom drawer, now sits on the mayor's desk...

Exposed...

It's not his first drink of the day.

The Administration infused his boy because of a petty crime... *a poster, for god's sake.* So, now the mayor feels the need to numb himself more than he has ever done. The thought of returning home, and to his distraught, teary-eyed wife, is unbearable.

He sips the velvet scotch, his nostrils infusing, his tongue savouring, and then the slow burn as it swishes into his gullet.

The heady warmth...

The onset of lightness.

Oh, he'll crash later. He knows it. But for now....

It surprised his staff that he returned to work so soon after his son's Eveningsong. But what else is there now but work?

Work and scotch.

Assistants everywhere tiptoe around him, doing everything they can to lighten his load. But he doesn't want to lighten it. He slams his hand on his desk, demanding the latest briefs: the one about new sewage pipes, and the ones about bicycle lanes, green space (always more green space), and the goddamn refugee settlement; its annexation and incorporation into Coal Town's tax system. He's read every single report through bleary eyes, struggling to take in each detail. Each syllable in every word. Concentrating. If he doesn't, then....

He sips more scotch.

He should go home to the wife; offer support during her suffering. Instead, he's apt to slap her. If only she hadn't doted so. Instead, if she had helped their son to fit in better; to conform.

But he too must share the blame. Too often, he ceded his paternal power to his wife, the boy's mother, to avoid confrontation. He asks himself how a man so pliable became the mayor of a place like Coal Town. It was fine when it was a sleepy village, where the most exciting thing was the breakdown of David Hannigan's tractor on the downtown bridge. It caused the town's first and only traffic jam of a half-dozen vehicles. The story made the front page of the local gazette.

But, in the past year, everything has changed. More climate refugees arrive each day, complicating things, gumming up the works. And the natives are restless.

The office door swings open and a pale, slender man steps in, the mayor's assistant.

"Go home, Mr. Mayor. Those briefs can wait another day. Your wife needs you."

The mayor looks up, groggy eyed from his work, at the one man he trusts above everyone else. It's he who keeps the place running. Truly. The mayor knows that next to a man such as his assistant; he's a figurehead only, a rubber stamp. It's his assistant who is the grease. Oh, the mayor does his bit. But he knows deep inside, without the assistant's crackerjack organizational ability, the place will fall into chaos.

The assistant spins the cap back onto the liquor bottle, then slips it into the bottom drawer with a wink.

"Come, Mr. Mayor. I'll give you a lift."

As pliable as ever, the mayor concedes.

He remembers little of the faltering journey from his desk to the assistant's car. And, lost in his thoughts, he remembers little of the slow drive through town until they stop at its lone traffic light; an initiative he spearheaded to protect children who cross the highway to access the only school. It cost a dear penny from the town's budget, but it bought him votes.

With the town expanding, they'll need more traffic lights. More complication.

He looks over at the assistant. He's a kind

man. Thus, the offer of a ride home. The mayor wonders if the assistant senses what he himself does—the rising tension in Coal Town. Not only because of burdensome climate refugees, but changing attitudes towards The Administration and The Beige.

After his son's infusion, there were those who came to him to express sympathy. But underlying it was quiet anger, resentment. Bitterness against The Administration's leaders, the bigwigs who, with each passing day, are more out of touch with the masses.

For god's sake, it was just a poster....

At first, he wondered if he was imbuing his own bitterness into what others told him. But no. He sensed the rising tension long before his son's Eveningsong. Towards him too, as an offshoot of The Administration. And if the pressure continues to rise, it'll detonate and there'll be anarchy again.

The assistant cranks the steering wheel, and his electric glides silently up to the curb in front of the mayor's house.

"Goodnight, Mr. Mayor...."

His face falls into one of his empathetic looks.

"Please consider taking time away. A couple of days, at least."

The mayor reaches over and squeezes the assistant's arm, slurring, "You're a good man, young sir. I'll consider it."

But as he steps out of the car and up onto

his porch, he knows he'll not consider time off. The work keeps him sane. He waves at the assistant as his car pulls away, disappearing into the night. Then he turns and peers through a window into the living room.

Desolate...

A single lamp burning...

The wife must've gone to bed.

Ever since the infusion, she cannot cope, and the mayor worries she may do something desperate. She's fallen into a bottomless depression and he, to his shame, has found little strength within himself to help. He braces himself before stepping through the door and into a waft of lemon-scented furniture polish. His wife must have spent the day cleaning. It's what she now does to keep herself from falling apart.

He climbs the stair. He must not wake her. If she's asleep, it's the first time since the infusion.

Tears will flow again when she looks at him, recognizing the same eyes, bred into their child. A father's square chin echoed in his son. The same peek in the hairline. Too many similar features in a boy who was, without a doubt, "his father's son."

He cracks the bedroom door. A shaft of light from the hall spills into the room. The bed is empty, its green velvet spread undisturbed. He switches on the light.

"My love...?"

He staggers across the room to the master bath, flipping a switch. Florescent bulbs above the sink flicker.

Deserted.

Stumbling from the bedroom, he reels down the stair and through the living room to the kitchen, switching on more lights.

Everything gleams...

The smell of Pine-Sol.

Looking from side to side, he notices the basement door is ajar.

"Oh, god...."

He lurches towards the door and hurls himself into darkness and down the stairs.

"My love...!"

Reaching the bottom of the stair, he glimpses something in the shadows and gasps.

There, slumped on a low stool with a drooping head, is his wife. She wears a simple black dress, and pinned above her heart, her grandmother's diamond brooch.

Reaching out, the mayor approaches and kneels in front of her, enfolding her hands in his. They feel icy.

As if only now sensing her husband, the mayor's wife raises her head, blinking.

The mayor looks upwards. There, tied to a rafter, is a rope fashioned from her collection of silk scarves.

The mayor's wife peers back at him, dried tears streaking her powdered face, her lipstick smeared. It's as though she's cried herself out and there's nothing left.

"I've been sitting here...."

Her voice drifts away, swallowed into silence.

The mayor pulls her into his chest, and for the first time, his tears flow.

Her voice, now only a whisper...

"How could they, lovebug? How could they...?"

***

Alistair Goodwin scrolls through his tablet, taking in the facts.

Results from tests related to the discovery of the MINI Cooper in the abandoned barn are conclusive. DNA and fingerprints prove the car belongs to Henry Chagall and Jack Parnell. It's clear they spent time in the barn, but there are scant clues as to their whereabouts now. The laying out of the shipping container homes, with cranes passing back and forth, destroyed other traces, except for two sets of footprints in the mud near the back of the barn, pointing toward the nearby rail line. Goodwin can imagine them following the train tracks. It's safer than the highway.

But in which direction? East or west.

Travelling east makes no sense. That would take them back in the direction they're fleeing. No. They must've travelled west, towards Coal Town and the Safehouse there. The same one The Administration bulldozed after Bateman killed the keeper. However, Jack Parnell and Henry Chagall were not among the elderly hidden in the house.

They may not have arrived there before the raid, or they somehow escaped. Either way, if they're not concealed somewhere else in Coal Town, they could be anywhere by now.

Goodwin scrolls on his tablet to another intriguing fact that twigged his internal radar; recent video capture from a drone surveying the highway outside Coal Town had detected something. Hidden in a grove of trees beside the highway was a black truck that appeared abandoned. Yet it was not, because stretched out underneath the truck, the drone's heat sensor detected a human form. Beyond the fact that it was a male, it is unclear from the red and orange heat patches in the sensor's image who this person is. However, his body length and estimated weight matches that of Yeorgi Stanovich, one of the suspected bombers.

More intriguing is that a street camera in Coal Town recorded the same black truck later in the day. However, the face of the driver didn't match that of Yeorgi Stanovich, as depicted in the wanted posters. This doesn't surprise Goodwin. The Administration still cannot rectify problems with facial recognition. Each time they solve one problem, thanks to Elizabeth Lowell's genius, the code reconfigures, causing another.

Clasping his hands behind his head, Goodwin leans back in his chair, gazing into space, his eyes narrowing as he falls into deep thought.

The world he inhabits dissolves, and he enters an imagined one where only known facts exist. He's no longer in his room, but in Coal Town. He places himself in the town square. Yet not a square at all, but a circle, a hub with streets radiating as spokes in all directions, north, south, east, and west. He imagines turning his body three-hundred-and-sixty degrees, taking in everything; the shops, the town hall, a church. Whenever he enters such trance-like states, the amount of detail he conjures up from an earlier visit to a particular location amazes him. He doesn't have a photographic memory, but one which is close to it.

He imagines The Group-of-Five into the picture.

Fact: given that he found evidence of Jack Parnell and Henry Chagall at the barn outside town, chances are they came to Coal Town. He pictures them walking one spoke towards the former Safehouse. When they discovered the place destroyed, did they flee? Or are they still in Coal Town? With the MINI Cooper out of commission, they have no vehicle. Not to say they didn't get another one from The Underground.

Fact, (but not really a fact): It is a conjecture that the person hidden under the black truck was Yeorgi Stanovich, and therefore only a possibility that he passed through Coal town.

Fact: There is no evidence of Elizabeth Lowell in Coal Town.

Fact: There is yet no evidence of Sasha

Dobrev in Coal Town.

As though sucked into a vacuum, the imagined world vanishes and Goodwin returns to his room in the real-world, dissatisfied with limited, disjointed facts. No full picture can yet fall into place.

Huffing, he stands and crosses his room to the window, looking out over the cityscape, projecting into supposition.

Suppose three out of the five had visited Coal Town. Why? Was it coincidental? Or is there a greater purpose? Too soon to know. However, he's certain of one thing. He must leave the city again and return to Coal Town. The group is westbound to the hypothetical haven, hidden somewhere in the northwest mountains, and full of insurgents, so they say. A place, The Administration says, does not exist. At least, The Administration has yet to find it. And if it ever does, they'll have no choice but to destroy it from above.

Targeted bombing.

***

The old man scrubs out his bucket in a deep sink and sanitizes his mop to keep it from mustiness. He puts them away for the last time. He's been part of janitorial services at the high-rise Thirty-Five Grange Road for decades, and he knows every single inch of the place, having cleaned every nook and niche; scrubbed every shit-stained toilet without complaint; mopped every floor. He's been a dedicated worker. And even though the executives who pass him each day view him as somehow less important, lowly; he's always given his best. He knows that without people like him, the world halts. Today he's meant to retire. And within three days, his Eveningsong.

He aligns all the cleaning products on the shelf, then rinses his scrub rags in disinfectant and hangs them out to dry, leaving everything shipshape for the new guy. The boy is young, and it's his first job. When the old man showed him the ropes, the kid spent much of the time scrolling through his electronic device, and not paying attention. The old man suspects that hardened bubble-gum under tabletops will go unscraped. Grime in corners will go without a deep scrub.

But all of that's management's problem now.

He slips on his long overcoat and takes one last look around. He's planned a trip to the roof. Checking out the view with a last cigarette of the day has become his Friday ritual, a way of tying up his workweek. Now, he'll tie up his life's work.

Climbing the stair, he passes through a door, letting it slam behind him and lock. As part of the maintenance team, he's one of the few people who has a key, so he needn't worry about the lock. Then he remembers. He's already handed over his heavy ring of keys to the new guy.

He steps up to the roof's edge and takes in the city's panorama. The sun is already setting. He's stayed long past shifts-end, wishing there could be just one more day of work. Wishing there were no Eveningsong and that there could be more years to a life. To his life.

But there won't be. The planet must survive, and The Administration expects him to do his bit.

He looks towards a large warehouse-type building across the street. The Administration works out of it. And the man in the beige uniform he often sees at 'The Un-Greasy Spoon.' The same Beige the old man stared down when he demanded papers.

But none of that matters now.

He takes out a cigarette and lights up. He inhales deeply and blows out the smoke, thinking, *My God, what a glorious sunset tonight....*

Then he bends down and reaches into a box which he had hauled up to the roof earlier in the day. He extracts a bottle from it and flicks his cigarette lighter again, igniting a rag crammed into its neck.

He lobs the flaming bottle through the air in a long arc, and it shatters on the rooftop of the building across the street.

Gasoline inside the bottle ignites, spreading fire.

Then another bottle, and another until flames engulf the entire surface of the roof.

Alarms sound.

From his perch, the old man watches as Administration workers in coloured jackets flee the burning building into the street...

Rats abandoning…

They look up towards him and point.

Soon he'll hear the sirens. Within minutes, fire trucks will arrive. Minutes are all he has before The Beige come for him; minutes left for his life. But he'll revel in the seconds ticking down.

The first van arrives, and The Beige scramble out. With rifles at the ready, they see him standing at the roof's edge, his long overcoat flapping in the breeze like Superman's cape. They clamber into the building. He imagines them charging up the stairs. He hears them ramming against the locked door leading to the roof.

This is it.

He's not a religious man. He doesn't believe in heaven or hell. Death is an end. Blackness.

They ram at the door again and then again. Soon it'll burst, and The Beige will flood through with their rifles and arrest him. Or kill him.

This is it.

He spreads his arms and leans into the wind…

Falling…

Falling…

Falling.

His last thought: *if only I could fly like Superman*.

But he cannot fly.

He hits.

His bones shattering like a bottle.

***

The Senior surveys the damage to his office. Water blasted from hoses has leaked into everything, shorting out the electrical system and destroying computers. His wall of bright surveillance screens is now black. Dead. Water has saturated the carpet. It already smells musty.

He steps out to the landing that rings the second level and scrutinizes the colour-coded pods below. The floor is a lake.

It was a situation he could not win. If he had not infused the mayor's son, he was open to attack from the jackals who condemn a two-tiered system. Infusing the boy has left him open to accusations of autocracy. Either way, the more desperate of the two groups were bound to rise from the throng and rebel with vehemence. Violence is the only way nowadays. Somewhere along the line there was a turning point, an end to civil protest, an end to civility all together.

The elderly man who threw himself from the rooftop after setting the fire had nothing left to lose. He was due for infusion within days, having neared his sixtieth birthday. He had set out to make his ultimate statement a spectacular one. And it was. It'll take days to move the operation to temporary premises and gear up again. And weeks, if not months, to refurbish the scorched and waterlogged building.

Whether using a pipe bomb to blow up an

Amphorium, or unsophisticated Molotov cocktails to set fires, the rebellious resort to using the readiest tools to press their point. And they're everywhere. Sometimes those like The Group-of-Five, at other times, a single man like the arsonist. There's no telling when or where they'll strike next. They've lost the purpose: the survival of the planet, and therefore humankind. What started out as altruism has devolved into partisan camps. Each dying for their own cause.

Each dying for the right to live.

The Senior makes his way to the corkscrew stair and descends to the main floor. In his gumboots, he wades through the shallow lake. One of the Molotov cocktails had crashed through a skylight and set off the sprinkler system long before firefighters aimed hoses at the roof. It was a deluge. Simple burning bottles, the cause. And a willingness to die within days of a prescribed infusion date. A desperate man taking control of his end. The Senior cringes at the thought that this is not the end of the man's example. Others will follow. But there's no turning back now. To change course would send a message that all infusions that came before were for naught.

He steps into the street as Alistair Goodwin arrives, ducking under a long strand of yellow tape surrounding the area. He extends his hand to him.

"Goodwin…"

"Senior."

Alistair scans the scene as workers wheel

water pumps into place.

"What a mess."

"There's a lake inside."

"Do you know anything about the man?"

The Senior holds his tablet out to Goodwin. He cringes at the image, recognizing the dead man as the old man he knows from the diner. The picture shows him lying on top of the blue sedan where he landed; wrapped in a blanket of metal folds, benign, as though in a deep sleep; dreaming. The Senior's voice snaps Goodwin into the present.

"I'm putting details together now."

He hates the details. They'll paint a picture of a human being. One who had a family; loved ones who'll suffer and ask themselves how someone they knew all their lives could do such a thing. Or perhaps this will not surprise them. They expected it. Either way, The Senior is about to paint a picture of a three-dimensional individual in shades of grey.

In his career, he can't recall a time when a perpetrator was completely evil. There's always a shred of light somewhere. He hates the light: a grandfather who loved his grandchildren, took them to the park to play, never forgot birthdays and was always ready with a gift at Christmas. Played Santa. Went to church. Widowed. Loved his wife. Spent his life contributing to society until his balance tipped and he rebelled.

Better if the culprit was completely dark. If so, The Senior could sleep at night. But he doesn't sleep anyway because he knows The Administration itself is shades of grey. Not evil. But not fully good.

"I hear you're going back to Coal Town, Goodwin."

"Yes. I suspect The Group-of-Five is heading west. Possibly to The Haven."

"It doesn't exist, poor fools."

"But they believe it does. And they believe it's west. I'll see if I can pick up traces in Coal Town. We know there were at least two of the group there, if not three."

"We're setting up temporary quarters. Stay connected. I need to know what you find out."

"Yes, Sir."

With this, Goodwin ducks back under the yellow tape, stepping over a strangle of drainage hoses as he makes his way to his car.

The Senior startles at the sound of the water pumps roaring into action.

He watches as Goodwin drives away, knowing he had just told him an outright lie.

***

Bateman toys with a pile of paperclips, linking them together in a long chain; a chain that shackles him to his desk. After the controversial incidents around the Safehouse and the mayor's son, The Administration busted him down to desk duty; to shuffling documents and playing with paperclips. He feels victimized, like a child sent to his room to keep him out of trouble. But a wink and a nod from The Senior assures him it won't be for long; just until the situation settles down. The problem is there's no sign of it settling. Feverish anger in the city and in places like Coal Town continue to rise.

He decides it's time for an early lunch. No one will care if he skips out fifteen minutes before noon. Rising from his desk, he meanders towards a door leading to the street. Nobody looks up from their work. No one appears to care if he comes or goes. He calls out to a pockmarked, bespectacled man.

"Hey, Billy. Early lunch…?"

Billy barely looks up from his work.

"Sorry man. No can do.…"

Even though Bateman waits, Billy offers no reason. Not, *"I've got to finish these reports.…"* Not, *"I'm working against the clock.…"*

Nothing.

Bateman feels bitter about how Billy has formed a dislike of him. It hasn't always been this way. There was a time when he and Billy had a workable friendship. But not now.

His career hasn't turned out the way he'd planned or hoped. Growing up, he had dreams of popularity. But somewhere along the line, the universe shifted against him. No matter how hard he tried to be a part of the "in-group," they always viewed him as uncool. It felt to him like destiny. At first, he didn't see it. But when the light switched on and he realized it, he strove even harder to make himself acceptable. This only worsened the problem, opening the door for the unscrupulous to manipulate him. He thought his situation would change once he joined The Beige. But no. All his attempts to take charge have led to bad choices.

He never should've put a bullet through the old woman's head. He'd adopted an aggressive posture in The Beige, believing it was his duty. His right.

As he steps from the harshly air-conditioned building to the street, he squints at the sun, allowing its heat to penetrate his skin. By mid-afternoon, the air will stifle. But for now, it's perfect. He decides he'll grab a sandwich from the vegan deli and find a bench in the cool of a wide-spreading tree in the town square.

Later, he bites into the sandwich with its layers of tofu and grilled vegetables, thinking how the extra hot mustard makes the thing tolerable. He sucks at his yogurt shake, tasting chemical strawberry before brain-freeze sets in.

A chickadee flits onto the bench beside him, expecting fallen crumbs from the bread roll. Bateman plucks out tiny bits and extends his hand. Without fear, the chickadee flutters onto his flattened palm and pecks. Bateman's lips curl as he watches the fragile little creature. He strains to not move and to scare it away. There, in the shade, with a chickadee pecking at his meager offering, he wonders if nature is healing after all. If the measures The Administration has taken —Eveningsong—are working. He wonders too if, when his time comes, he'll sacrifice himself for the good of all.

He sniffs the air. There's a sweetness to it he's never sensed before. Indeed, for unfathomable reasons, today he feels a heightened sense. Colours seem brighter. Tastes are stronger. Sounds clearer. He watches all the people passing through the square as he sits on the bench, noticing the smallest detail: freckles across a child's nose, fallen strands from a woman's pinned up hair, a slightly in-turned foot which has worn down the heel on a left shoe more than the right. And a man in a baseball cap stepping out of the alley; the same alley where he took down the mayor's son. Then, as though changing his mind, the man recedes back into its shade, avoiding the intenseness of the sun, no doubt. Bateman has a sense of being a part of all things. It floods into him, overwhelming him. Dizzying him.

Then he sees it.

A black pickup truck parked in the square. A man wearing a plaid shirt at its steering wheel.

One of The Group-of-Five.

Yes, he's certain of it.

Slowly, he rises from the bench and the chickadee flutters away.

Locking eyes with the driver of the truck, he moves across the square, instinctively feeling for the gun that is always on his hip since taking the beige. But not today. The Senior made him turn it in when he busted him down to desk duty.

He sees a sad grin spread across the face of the man in the plaid shirt; pained, as though he's suffering. The man reaches into his shirt pocket, taking out a small device. Bateman, with his heightened sense, knows at once what it is. He cries out to the people in the square as he turns to run.

But then a thunderous boom echoes throughout the square.

Shop windows shatter.

Debris spews in all directions, penetrating flesh as people fall to the ground, blown off their feet.

A massive fireball consumes the truck and its driver. Its orange plume balloons out, and in an instant it incinerates Bateman.

CHAPTER 9

Sasha staggers along the alley in shock, his ears ringing. Had he not stepped back when he did, shrapnel from the blast would have severely injured him, or killed him. Still, he'd felt the impact. At first, he was excited to see Yeorgi's pickup. But when he stepped from the alley and saw an officer in beige sitting on a nearby bench, he'd pulled his cap down over his eyes and receded into the shadows.

Then the detonation.

Now an incessant ringing in his ears.

Pressing his hands against the sides of his head, he reels. A man running away from the square reaches out to steady him.

"Are you alright…?"

Sasha peers back at him, bleary-eyed. *What's he saying…?* Sasha can only hear the man's muffled voice. Persistent…

"Are you *alright*…?"

Sasha pulls away and leans back against a brick wall, steadying himself as he nods. He hears his own voice responding. Barely audible. Gasping. Oddly detached…

"Yes. Yes. I'm okay...."

The stranger turns from him and runs to assist a wounded woman, struggling to her feet.

Sasha digs his fingers into the bricks to hold himself up as he pulls himself back along the alley, peering through the smokiness.

Shattered windows...

Cracked buildings...

The wide-spreading tree, ablaze...

Bloodied bodies on the ground. Others struggling to their feet, scarred...

Approaching sirens sounding through the muffle.

Sasha's mouth falls open as he looks towards the remnants of Yeorgi's truck, and to a charred body nearby: the remains of the man in beige. He struggles to put together jumbled thoughts.

"Where do I go...?"

"What do I do...?"

An image of Marta and Little Robert fights its way into his scrambled mind. Although he knows they may be miles away by now at the farm site, he fears for their safety. With a last glance at the carnage, he turns and flees back down the alley.

Meanwhile, Marta's truck had only reached the outskirts of the town when she heard the blast. She'd slammed on the brakes and looked back over her shoulder towards the rising smoke. In the seat next to her, Little Robert had looked at her wide-eyed.

"What was that...?"

Now, Marta spins the steering wheel and speeds back into the town, her instincts conflicted. On the one hand, there was an explosion. Who knows what may come next? Better to flee with her son to a safe distance. On the other, a panicked urge to go back to where she had dropped off the man, they call Big Robert... *"Please, God, let him be safe...."*

She'd awakened with a start that morning and found him sitting at the table in the main room sipping instant coffee, looking lost in his thoughts. Right away, she could tell this was the end for them. He'd kept his promise to get her and Little Robert to safety, and now it was time for him to leave. Without speaking, she'd emptied a packet of coffee crystals into a mug and poured water from the kettle, still steaming on the hotplate, then sat.

Across the table, Sasha had peered out the window at the golden morning light, struggling with what he wanted to express; the words he wanted to put together to make things less awkward. Marta knew there could never be the right words at a time like this. Although she herself felt a mixture of emotion, she knew she had no right to ask the man she had known such a brief time to stay. Finally, it was she who broke the silence.

"I'll drive you into town...."

"You understand why I have to leave."

"But where will you go? What will you do?"

"I'm almost certain that was…." He'd caught himself before he spoke the name.

He needn't have held back. The Administration had matched all the faces of The Group-of-Five with their names on posters plastered to walls everywhere. Marta knows his real name is Sasha Dobrev, not Robert like her son. She knows the name of the man he's looking for is Yeorgi.

"What if it wasn't him? What if he's long gone? What then?"

"I don't know. But I can't stay here. It's unsafe for you and Little Robert. The Administration is ruthless with anybody who aids or abets. It's not safe."

Even though it had been mere days since Marta had fled her burning town, it felt like a lifetime. She'd recognized Sasha the instant he washed the soot from his face, and in the same instant she decided not to expose him for what he was: one of the Amphorium bombers. She was sympathetic to the cause. Besides, the bombing at The Amphorium didn't kill anyone. This new bomb, however, at the centre of the town at mid-day would have, surely.

Now, as she drives towards the smoke, she wonders if the man her son knows as Big Robert had anything to do with it.

Screaming emergency vehicles force her to the side of the road as they pass. She sits there, lost, confused, reminded of a tragic film she once saw, which ends with a shattered woman standing on a street corner, unable to decide left or right.

It's Little Robert's voice that brings her back to her senses.

"There he is...!"

Refocusing, she peers out from the truck and sees him. There, among a stream of the wounded flowing away from the town square, is Sasha, looking dazed, aimless.

Marta springs from the truck and runs to him. Fate has made the choice. As she nears him, he seems to come to. She opens her arms to him, and he falls into them. She wrestles him into the truck, next to Little Robert.

Trembling, Sasha pulls the boy into his chest.

Climbing inside beside them, Marta spins the wheel and together, they all speed away.

***

Wind!
Raging...
Destructive.

It comes from nowhere, sweeping across the prairie, flattening the wheat. Anything not tied down: a wheelbarrow, outdoor furniture, and a barbeque blows away. There's no time to set loose the animals from the corrals; no time to lead others from the barn. Only time to flee to the cellar as walls rattle, shutters rip from their hinges, and the front porch gives way, splintering into oblivion.

The farmer's son huddles with his father and mother against the basement wall, listening to the sounds of a house wrested away. First the roof, then walls and windows. Shattering glass. He prays that the floor above them will hold, and rubble won't bury them alive. He thinks about the livestock and losing things: black and white family portraits hanging in the living room; grandparents and great grandparents who managed the farm before them. And what may seem trivial to others, his collection of postcards; pictures of places to which he never travelled but has always dreamt about. All of it taken in the deafening howl.

He looks to the other side of the basement at the strangers his parents allowed into their home: this Elizabeth, Henry, and Jack huddling together; fearful of the roar. All a part of The Group-of-Five; a part of the rebellion. Is this destruction God's punishment for taking them in? He wonders about Elizabeth; someone not much older than him. Yet she has sided with Henry and Jack; men from the generation who didn't take care, who didn't change the way they lived until this, a wind with a freight train's growl, thundering through the living room.

Anger flushes through him. His face reddens. Looking at his parents, he wonders how they could've taken in these strangers when they know that, because of people such as Jack and

Henry, their own son has no future.

Then, abrupt silence...

The wind subsides...

Only the sound of water trickling into the basement from broken pipes...

Only the sound of their breathing.

He cocks a wary ear.

"It's over... I think."

He follows his father up the stairs, where they push open the basement door, heaving at the debris which the wind has blown up against it. They and the others crawl from the cellar into utter destruction. The roof and half of the second floor are gone. Now there is a sky. A bed in one of the upstairs bedrooms teeters precariously over a jagged edge, threatening to topple into the living room.

The farmer and his wife scan the remains of their home. Steadfastly, they push down all their feelings as if they've always known it was only a matter of time.

Nothing left in its place...

Everything is a jumble.

The farmer's wife reaches out and squeezes her husband's hand. But it's too much for him. If he holds her hand longer, feelings will rise from his gut, pour from his eyes. He lets go her hand as their son stumbles past them through the wreckage to a heavy oak sideboard, only slightly askew from its place against the wall in what used to be the dining room. He slides open a drawer and takes out a well-worn photo album and a stack of postcards. Only then does he sink to his knees and weep.

Later, when he surveys the yard with his father, there are dead chickens. Miraculously, two or three have survived. God knows how. But the horse he loves lays prostrate on the ground huffing, grunting. Flotsam from the obliterated barn has impaled him, leaving him battered and bloodied. Wheezing. Dying.

Somewhere under the wreckage is a rifle, which could end its misery.

But then the pitiable moaning ends...

One last blinking eye...

One last steaming breath.

Then, from a distance, a voice...

"It's still here...!"

Elizabeth comes round from the east side of the house. The wind had come from the west, and the part of the house left standing had protected her vehicle. Other than scratches and dents from flying rubble, her electric is still functional. Unlike the farmer's truck, which the indiscriminate wind rolled over and over into the field.

After a sorrowful gaze at his devastated land, the farmer turns to Elizabeth.

"You'd better go...."

"We can't leave you like this."

"Help will come. You can't be here when it does."

"But..."

"Go...."

He tilts his head towards Jack and Henry.

"Get yourself and these men to safety. It's all right."

The farmer's son, his brow furrowing, gapes at his father. He cannot for his life understand why his father makes the choices he does. Siding with the rebels has endangered his family. Now, he is determined to save them from authorities who would discover them when they come to assess the damage. The son's confusion and his anger deepening, as if these strangers, and they alone, caused the ruin all around him.

Elizabeth reaches out, cupping the farmer's hands in hers.

"Thank you for everything, brother. For taking us in. Sheltering us."

As they drive away, Jack looks back through the rear window at the farmer and his family as they recede into the distance. He'd never even learned their names. But that's the way of things in the Safehouses. People sharing what they have from their meagre food, a roof, a bed. But no names. Never a history.

Elizabeth's car speeds along the highway.

Jack and Henry look out over the fields. What was once waving wheat is now a straw mat. And as they near the outskirts of the town, they see it didn't escape the wrathful wind. People crawl from their basements to pick through the wreckage and look on in shock as they salvage what they can from their collapsed houses.

Elizabeth navigates the main street, maneuvering around mounds of scrap. Clearly only buildings constructed out of concrete, stone or brick still stand: the town hall, the school, the post office.

One wall of a church is now a mass of rubble, exposing the inside to the outside like a gutted fish. A couple dozen of its congregants have gathered at the site. Kneeling amongst the debris, they reach out to heaven with gratitude for their survival and an imploration for grace. Someone strikes up a hymn, and the others join in…

> *On a hill far away*
> *Stood an old rugged cross.*
> *The emblem of suffering and strife….*

People are too distressed, too caught up in their losses that few note Elizabeth and the others as they traverse the town to its western boundary. When they arrive there, they gaze out again at the vastness of the flatlands, hoping that against all odds, the car's battery will last until they reach the next Safehouse, the next charging station.

Then to where the landscape undulates into foothills, finally rising to commanding mountains.

To The Haven.

***

Little Robert crawls onto the bed and curls up next to Big Robert, who sleeps deeply. He listens to Big Robert's breathing.

Steady...

In and out. In and out...

Little Robert will be his teddy bear. Just like the one he cuddled when he was afraid of the dark. Before the fire took the bear, it used to make Little Robert feel comforted. Safe.

Or he'll be like the puppy he once knew. Instinctively sensing Little Robert's distress, he would come to him, silent, sweet, and lay his chin on Little Robert's knee. Sad-eyed and empathetic. No yips, no whimpers, no puppy's words. Just silent support. Yes, Little Robert decides, that's what he'll be for Big Robert. A puppy.

Something terrible has happened in the world; an explosion to add to the losses from the fire. He caught snippets in whispers between his mother and Big Robert, and he's smart enough to understand that there's a connection between Big Robert and the explosion. More so than for other people in the town. Still, this man makes him feel safe. After the fire, Big Robert had guided him and his mother to the security of this tiny house. Now, Little Robert sees the way his mother looks at Big Robert, sensing that she too needs him; wants him in her life.

Little Robert never knew his real father. He doesn't know the entire story, but he gleans from whispers that the man walked out even before seeing the son he helped create.

Frustratingly, although he's intuitive, there's

so much he doesn't understand about grownups. But, like a puppy, he senses. He senses this good man with a good heart has grownup troubles. Right now, Big Robert needs him. He knows this because of the way the man had pulled him into his chest in the truck after the explosion. Like a teddy bear.

And so, he decides, he will offer him the comfort of a teddy bear, and a puppy's sympathy.

Sasha inhales deeply as he awakens with suddenness from the darkness of a dreamless sleep, taking in the child's enquiring eyes watching him.

The child's voice, soft. A whisper…

"Hi…."

Sasha's voice, dry, raspy…

"Hello…."

"You been sleepin' a long time. Did you sleep good…?"

Sasha wonders what "a long time" means. And he wonders how long the boy has been watching him.

Little Robert jumps off the bed excitedly and disappears around the partition that separates the bed from the kitchen area.

"Momma, he's awake…!"

Marta pokes her head around the partition, chirping cheerfully.

"Hello there. Welcome back to the land of the…"

She catches herself.

"Are you hungry...?"

"How long have I been out?"

"A day and a half."

Sasha sits up, bewildered. He remembers collapsing on the bed after the explosion...

Yes...

There was an explosion...

Yeorgi.

He remembers closing his eyes for what was to be just a minute. Now this. A day and a half have passed with no memory of it. Like a blink. Time without no remembered dreams.

And now, a bursting bladder.

He crawls off the bed and heads to the bathroom.

He purges himself, then strips and steps into the shower, letting icy water stream over him. Cold enough to startle him; to wake him.

Yes. There was an explosion.

Yeorgi, dead. Others, dead or wounded.

The man in beige... charred....

It should not have come to this. It was never the original plan. No one was supposed to die. The intention was to destroy an Amphorium and make a statement; challenge people to think about what the world had become.

Each in the group had suffered at the hands of The Administration, but they never intended to cause more suffering; only to protest; awaken people to how askew things had become; how far off track from the original law of Each-one-for-

Everyone.

How corrupt the system.

As he stands there in the flow of frigid water, he reflects on how extreme Yeorgi was, compared to others in the group. His anger and his psychic pain ran deeper. Especially his anger. Is that what drove him to detonate a second bomb? To blow himself up in a village square.

He steps from the shower and towels off. He glimpses his face in the mirror, taking in the shadow of a two-day growth. Under it all, a once-fresh face now looks haggard. And not even a razor to shave with; having lost his knapsack holding all his possessions in the alley after the bomb.

Stepping from the bathroom, he breathes in the aroma of fresh chicory coffee. Breakfast is ready, and Little Robert is already eating his cereal. Still feeling lightheaded and weak, Sasha stumbles to a chair and sits.

At the hotplate, Marta reaches for a fork...

"The Administration gave us powdered eggs. Scrambled good enough...?"

"Perfect."

He watches as Marta sprinkles salt and pepper into the eggs and whips them into a froth.

Sitting there, seeing her prepare the breakfast, sudden emotion overwhelms him, more than at any other time in his life. He had sensed a growing bond with Marta and the boy in the days after the fire. But this simple act of her making eggs and buttering toast somehow solidifies it.

And the boy eating his cereal. The same inquisitive eyes which he wakened to, now watching him over a spoon raised to his lips. Sasha blinks to stem the tide flooding into his own eyes. How can he explain to the boy the powerful flash just now? Everything falling together with a shocking suddenness.

And the overpowering love.

Love for him and his mother.

Oh, how he wants to stay with them forever; make their lives beautiful.

But, because of choices made long before he met them, he must leave.

Marta tips the frying pan, dumping the scrambled eggs onto a plate in front of Sasha.

"Sorry, there's no *faconbacon*. But there *is* toast."

"It's enough for now."

"You haven't eaten in almost two days. I'll go to the village and try to score some fruit. I'm also gonna apply for that server's job at the café."

She tilts her head, taking him in. He still seems lost. He's unaware that twice during his coma he got up from the bed to wander about the room, somnambulant; his eyes not seeing, before returning to the bed to continue his sleep. It was his personal reaction to the trauma, and it worried her. She'd considered calling a doctor, but she knew she couldn't. And now, sitting there watching him eat the eggs, wonders if he'll ever completely come back to himself.

"You'll stay, won't you?"

Taken aback, Sasha looks up from his eggs. But Marta continues.

"To take care of Little Robert, I mean. While I go to the village."

"Of course…. It wouldn't be wise for me to step out, anyway. Not now. Not until things settle down."

Marta had yet to hear any news around the blast. But authorities would be on the lookout for anyone else from The Group-of-Five who might be in the area, surely. Yes. It's best that he stays inside.

A smile breaks across Sasha's lips as he watches Little Robert play with his cereal.

"Besides, I can think of nothing better than being with Little Robert right now, watching him spell words with his Alpha-Bits."

Little Robert looks up from his bowl.

"Look… I spelled puppy. See…?"

Sasha takes in the bowl. Sure enough, there's the word, floating in milk… *puppy*.

Marta reaches for her purse.

"I shouldn't be long."

She plans to keep her ear cocked for any bits of news she can pick up about the investigation around the bombing and whether authorities are searching for any others connected to it.

Minutes later, as she drives towards the village, she reflects on her conflicted mind. On the one hand, she wants Sasha to stay, but she knows the danger. Sasha's right. The Administration has zero-tolerance for those who aid and abet. They won't think twice about taking Little Robert away from her, then infusing her for betraying the law of Each-one-for-Everyone.

CHAPTER 10

Socks…
Men's briefs…
T-shirts…
Toiletries, and a razor.

Goodwin scrutinizes various articles spread out before him. These are contents of a knapsack abandoned in an alley off the village square. It appears to be the same knapsack seen slung over the shoulder of a man caught on a security cam. Positioned near the site of the explosion, the cam recorded the killing of innocent citizens and Officer Bateman. When investigators first discovered the discarded knapsack, they feared it may contain another bomb. But no. Only these personal items.

When he returned to Coal Town from the city, Goodwin had intended to follow the scant trail of The Group-of-Five, believing one or more of them had passed through the village. He did not expect that an explosion in the square would add to his investigation. But it has.

He received news of the bombing while on the road. After a call from The Senior, he pulled over his electric and watched live coverage on his monitor. It was devastating, sickening. People were dead. There was chaos. So many unknown facts. He knew the local administration would cordon off the area and would start putting pieces together. But he intended to take over the investigation himself at once.

Of course, there was blowback. However, he's now in charge, and he now sits in a massive semi-truck trailer bursting with technology, overseeing a busy team of data crunchers. And scrutinizing socks, underwear, and a razor.

The Administration hauled in the trailer to aid the investigation. Painted black, it's intimidating. It adds gravitas; makes it known to the citizenry that The Administration is serious about hunting down everyone connected to the heinous bombing, and that they will mete out maximum punishment.

Punching a button, Goodwin calls up footage from the security cam. Big data has stored all the cam's information up to where the blast destroyed it. The footage shows an unidentified man stepping from an alley leading off the square just before the detonation. He has the knapsack. The man pulls down his cap, obscuring his face. And as if fearing someone in the square has recognized him, he quickly steps back into the alley. Then the truck explodes. Goodwin winces at the horrific images of shrapnel peppering passers by.

People fall to the ground...

A fiery plume swallows Bateman...

The camera goes dead.

The unidentified man in the alley was not among the corpses or the critically wounded. He, like others who survived the blast, must have fled the square, giving no thought to the knapsack he left behind.

Goodwin recalls one anecdote he heard from that day. A story about a woman, blown out of her sandals. She did not think to retrieve them before she fled. Fearing for her life, she escaped barefoot. Then, in a bizarre turn, she arrived at the offices of The Administration to see if anyone had found her shoes at the scene. As if they were the most important of her possessions, her lost children. She was still barefoot, and clearly in shock. However, the staff dutifully noted a description: women's leather sandals—size eight, white—and then watched as the poor woman drifted from the office in a daze.

To this day, no one has come to the station to enquire about a lost knapsack, in shock or otherwise.

There was no wallet holding I.D. in the bag. No driver's licence or Citizen's Card. No cell phone. There are no identifiers of any kind. But there are other ways which may help name the owner: DNA testing. The same type of tests performed on the remains of the driver of the truck.

Goodwin reflects on drone footage he had studied before. Its heat sensor showed a blurry red and orange image of a man hiding under a truck in a grove of trees on the outskirts of town. The same truck blown to smithereens in the square. Its driver now confirmed as Yeorgi Stanovich, a member of The Group-of-Five.

He puts together the facts he knows. The unidentified man from the alley is about the same age, height, and estimated weight as another member of the group: Sasha Dobrev. Any DNA unwittingly left behind on the knapsack or razor; hair, skin flakes, or blood spots may confirm it. Although it's a slow process, Goodwin is patient. He'll wait for results. Fact by fact; he'll put together a full picture. Step by step, he comes closer to those he's looking for. He's certain he'll track them down. It's just a matter of time. He loves putting together facts. It's what he did when he worked for the oil industry. Before it collapsed. Before he refused to take seriously his son's admonitions that the data he collected to enable his company to drill for more oil were contributing to the death of the planet. He squelches the twinge in his gut from remembrance and focuses on evidence related to the goal at hand.

Fact: one of The Group-of-Five is now dead. Fact: the MINI Cooper in the barn shows that two others, Jack Parnell and Henry Chagall, passed through Coal Town. They may still be here. If DNA proves the knapsack belongs to Sasha Dobrev, he, too, was in Coal Town and may still be here. He knows nothing yet of the whereabouts of Elizabeth Lowell.

Each member of the group has been clever. Either they're not using any technology they have, or they destroyed all of it before fleeing. There are no cell phone pings. There are no on-line connections. Nothing. There can be no geolocation. They have mostly avoided security cams and drone cams, which means they avoid large metropolitan areas where there's vast coverage.

Elizabeth Lowell has discombobulated facial recognition. Each day, The Administration comes closer to unravelling her code. And they continue to gather intelligence about the vast underground, strung out across the country, which aid the terrorists.

It surprises Goodwin that an underground exists at all. The law of Each-one-for-Everyone is working, isn't it? The earth is healing...isn't it?

He brings himself back to another question, which he continues to ponder. Is there a reason that at least four of the group passed through Coal Town?

Is it coincidence, or is it because this town is on the road to the mythical Haven?

***

"Condolences..."

"Huh…? Oh, the bastard you mean…."

Katarina's harsh response startles The Senior, and he withdraws his outstretched hand. All said and done, Yeorgi Stanovich was her husband and the father of her child. As evil as he was, he had died a horrible death. She sidles halfway through the door, aloof, uncaring.

She has extruded herself into a stretchy cotton-candy-pink dress, and at once The Senior pegs her as a certain type of woman; flirtatious, when necessary, hard, and crass if needs be. He's seen it before; a cliché. And he wonders why people like her can never see it for themselves.

The dress accentuates her full breasts and, sadly, her rolling waistline. She's the type of woman who was once beautiful, but who is now succumbing to the outcomes of an indolent life spent mostly on the make; the kind that still relies on once potent wiles which, in The Senior's view, now seem pathetic in a woman her age. She's no longer an ingenue, although she likes to play it that way. Her makeup, which, in years past, may have highlighted pretty features, is now overdone as she tries vainly to cover lines etched into her skin. She looks plastic; a kewpie doll, her rosebud lips freshened with deep red just before stepping into the room.

She leans into The Senior and shoots him a coquettish look, either to endear herself to him and distance herself from the man she refers to as "the bastard," or a subtle sign that she's on offer. She's smart enough to leave one guessing. Especially someone from The Administration. Still, it's her opening gambit; always on the make. It's what she knows.

But The Senior isn't buying. He returns a blank stare as he opens the door wider and ushers her into the room.

Her eyes hardening with disappointment at his lack of interest, Katarina scans the surroundings.

"This room's a lot nicer than the one at the last interrogation."

"This is not an interrogation, Mrs. Stanovich…"

"It's not *Mrs*. We got divorced."

"Of Course."

"You can call me Katarina. *Kat*, if you like. Friends call me Kat."

There's that coquettishness again.

Again, The Senior isn't buying. He returns another blank stare.

Katarina drifts about the room, taking in everything, dragging her fingers over surfaces.

"Comfortable sofa for me. An easy chair for you. Lighting, not so harsh as in the last room, thank God. Better for the skin."

A sideways glance at The Senior. If she expected even a tepid grin at her mild joke, it's not there.

"Hmmm…. Coffee table with a box of tissues. In case the trauma of it all makes me cry...?" A slight grin. "No two-way mirror this time. But a camera in the upper corner..."

She wiggles her fingers at it.

"You're recording me, *arentcha*... Yes. Always recording even though I'm no longer a suspect. Because I'm a victim, right? A cold interrogation room for suspected accessories to a crime. A comfortable room like this for people you think are victims. Am I right? Because I *am* a victim, you know. As much as anybody else." Her words have the bite of accusation. "By now, you must think I'm a victim, otherwise I'd be in the other room. Or even a cell waiting for an infusion. Am I right? I know how it works."

She plops onto the sofa, one leg crossed over the other, turned away slightly, ready to move on: unwilling to waste valuable time or sexual energy on someone who's not playing.

"So, what do you want? Why am I here...?"

"Katarina...."

Her face sags into a pout. The Senior throws her a bone. It'll make her compliant.

"*Kat*... this is not an interrogation. I thought we could just chat a little. I thought you could help me understand why Mr. Stanovich would do such a thing as to..."

"Blow himself up?" She huffs. "I'm not a psychiatrist."

"Of course not. But you lived with the man."

"Only long enough to pop out his baby."

The Senior sits back in his chair. *His* baby.

Not my baby. Not our baby. But *his* baby. The Senior makes a mental note to have child protection services check in from time to time...

Katerina shifts, settling back into the corner of the sofa.

"He was a hothead. Everything made him angry. He listened to too much sad news on TV; watched too many YouTube videos of people just like him, who were just as angry as he was. That's how he connected with that... what're you calling it...?"

"The Group-of-Five...."

"Yeah, that. That's probably where he even learned how to build a bomb."

"Did you ever meet any of the people he interacted with?"

Katerina's shoulders sag and she lets out a long sigh, her head shaking slowly. She cannot believe what Trinket's father did; that he should go to such an extreme.

"He kept me out of it, I tell ya. Me and Yeorgi were on the outs for a long time. I mean, he paid his child support regular. But now what? The bastard left me under water and broke. Makin' people like you suspect I did somethin' wrong just 'cause I knew him; was married to him." She gazes into space. Lost. "Lookin' back, I shoulda known somethin' was up. I mean, there were signs. But that's only thinkin' back on it. It's easy lookin' backwards, isn't it?"

She's drifting. Thinking about signs that are

of no use to anyone now…

And about being under the water and broke…

And about his child, who is a constant reminder.

***

A dim corner of The Quails. Fashioned to look like a centuries-old English pub…

Crowded…

Orangey light through tinted leaded glass…

Tanqueray, tonic, ice, a lime wedge…

Ginni and Lila clink their glasses.

"To Bateman."

Dressed in their impeccable beige uniforms, they're seated on tufted leatherette chairs at a wobbly table, its surface swiped at with a mucky rag in haste to make way for them, but still sticky.

Others from The Beige crammed into the room, murmuring, sometimes a hardy laugh erupts out of the press of bodies. Uniformed men and women representing detachments from across the country crammed together. Overheated. Sweaty in saturated air, stinking of stale beer. Alcohol, while wearing the beige, only allowed after a funeral with full honours for the fallen.

For Bateman.

Ginni dips her fingertip into her drink, swirling the ice. After sucking away the liquid, she sips the drink as she scrutinizes Lila.

"He had a thing for you, you know."

"Yup...."

"He didn't think I knew it. But I could see. Just by the way he looked at you." She narrows her eyes. "You have a thing for him?"

"Nope...."

"Too bad. He was a good fuck."

Lila shudders.

"You're speaking ill of the dead."

"I said he was a *good* fuck. How is that speaking ill...?"

She drains the glass, savouring it in her mouth, then swallows.

"He was needy." She puckers her lips into a rosebud. "It made the foreplay last. I like that in a man."

Lila snorts, then sinks back into pensiveness.

"Horrible way to go, though...."

"Quick...."

Ginni focuses her eyes on an image floating in mid-air, visible only to her. Behind the brown eyes with green flecks and the dilating pupils, there's deep sadness. Loss. Not for something she had, but what she could've had...

If she'd allowed...

Let the wall down.

Lila breaks Ginni's trance.

"You had no genuine feelings for him then? It was just sex?"

"Haven't decided yet...."

She holds up her empty glass, catching the eye of the server who heads for the bar with her tray. It'll be her third gin. But it's not helping the way it usually does. Usually, she can feel the alcohol flattening her out after a tough day. But today she's all up and down.

After Bateman's shocking end, people are bound to reevaluate. Why should it be only now that she understands the nuance of their relationship? She didn't know until now—after gin and tonic number three—that her feelings ran deeper. Feelings she doesn't want. Not now. Especially because she knew too much about the man. Whatever virtues he had early on, he was no longer good. He perverted his power. And she wonders if that's where she's headed. The job forces her to develop a crust. Has it left her bereft of compassion? Where she reduces a man, she could've loved to a glib comment about a good fuck.

After the chaos of Reckoning, The Beige brought order. Calm. That's why she joined. But now it's all verging on disorder again. People hate The Beige.

It may only be the alcohol coursing through her synapses, but right now—in this moment—she feels like it's all for nothing. People say they believe that the law of Each-one-for-Everyone is working. That they're saving the earth... humankind. But, what with the rebellious blowing things up... blowing up Bateman... and the stories about floods and fires and blizzards in summer and devastating winds, it's difficult to believe that the earth isn't making war. It's angry; a living, fire-breathing, vengeful beast.

The server sets another Tanqueray and tonic in front of Ginni. She ponders its crystal clarity. The ice. The hubbub of the room, muffles and all the sweaty bodies disappear. Even Lila melts away. It's as though Ginni is falling into the glass, swimming in its frigid liquid. Thinking, if only Bateman had cut the macho act, she might've fallen for him; let herself love him. Even she, with her tough exterior, needs reaching out for. Not in a way that signals more rutting. But reassurance that there is no terrible end in store after hedonism; a price to pay after a good fuck and from the angry earth.

She drains the glass and holds it up to the server, who nods and heads for the bar again.

Lila's voice, softly…

"Maybe you should pull back a little."

"Pull back…!" There's angry irony in her slurred words. "Pull back…?"

She looks bleary-eyed across the table to Lila, who gazes back at her, an odd mixture of sympathy for the grieving and readiness to defend herself from a drunk, bouncing back and forth between belligerence and self-pity.

"Just saying…."

Ginni offers a reassuring smile; a smile that is an honest embrace.

"Just one more and I'm done. We're *all* done...."

***

Drip...
Clank.
Drip...
Clank.
Drip....
Droplets bead on the portable air-conditioner, which The Senior has jammed into a rotting window frame. They rain down into a metal pan placed on the ragged hardwood floor of his temporary quarters...

Drip...
Clank.
It makes it difficult to concentrate.

Refinishing the floors or finding a solution to the incessant dripping would be an admission that his unit may have to headquarter in these shabby surroundings longer than he'd hoped. After the firebombing, they scrambled to find a sizable space which could accommodate a large staff and its needs. And they've ended up in a dusty, moth-eaten warehouse, where brownouts are frequent. Securing new equipment to get back up and running was a mammoth task. All because of an old man and his rudimentary Molotov cocktails:

Drip...
Clank.

The Senior studies a spreadsheet outlining all the destruction from the bombing in Coal Town: the number of the dead, the wounded and the damage to buildings. The local mayor and his council will need support. Data also suggests there is rising resentment around the resettlement of climate refugees from the north. Another situation which will require support. But since the infusion of the mayor's son at The Senior's instigation, he wonders if he's the best person to make inroads with the mayor. The entire situation is a political nightmare. He's uncertain if the mayor intends to run in the upcoming election. It would be better if he didn't. Having kept his ear to the tom-toms, The Senior senses that after the death of his son, the mayor may lean towards support for the rebellion.

If it comes to it, The Administration could provide the media with certain big data which may influence backing for another candidate. With the current mayor gone, and the installation of someone more friendly to The Administration, they could minimize problems.

More than anything, they must make certain that Yeorgi Stanovich does not become a martyr to the cause.

After the bombing, The Senior ordered Stanovich's ex-wife, Katarina, in for another round of questioning. She admitted Stanovich had visited her days prior to his suicide. She made every attempt to clarify that she had no sympathy for "the bastard." And she denounced him up and down as a bad husband, a terrible father and worse, an ineffective lover, painting him as impotent "with a small cock." She implied that now that Stanovich had committed his "selfish act," she had no way of supporting "his" child. Beyond facts, The Administration already knows—the man's association with Sasha Dobrev, for instance—Katarina had little information to add to the profile that is Yeorgi Stanovich. She was a dead end. The Senior viewed her as a thoroughly distasteful creature and was happy to see the back of her. But not before she implied The Administration owed her something for her negligible information. *"After all, I now gotta support the bastard's kid all by myself, don't I ...?"*

Before the next drip, The Senior empties the overflowing water pan into a bedraggled philodendron. Cherise had dragged it in to warm up the place. *"You're housed in this ramshackle for now, but it needn't be completely dreadful."* For his part, The Senior couldn't care less. He prefers function over form, and certainly over décor.

He takes in his wall of monitors, all new and set up at great expense. Images flicker in perpetual motion across each screen. Even he, a Senior in a sub-branch of The Administration, can call up any cam he wants, anywhere in the world. It's a voyeur's dream.

From his ergonomic chair, he can sip his chicory and take in everything from the mundane to the prurient; from prostitutes giving blowjobs to John's in back alleys in Taiwan, to those in The Administration conducting their grift. Everyone's in on it. Even The Beige, who knows someone's watching and should therefore know better than to perpetuate their own corrupt acts in plain view.

But, nowadays, who or what is not in plain view?

The Group-of-Five, that's what. Now a group of four.

His eyes flick from one monitor to the next. If only he could see something amongst it all, a clue to their whereabouts. But there's just too much to look at; to take in.

After so many years of studying his monitors, he's seen it all. The prurient has become mundane; the salacious details only useful when trying to strong-arm someone.

If only someone on the team could bring him something, a snippet. Anything. But, given that Elizabeth Lowell was once on the inside, he no longer knows who to trust. Are more sympathizers planted on the inside? His eyes flick to a particular monitor, its security camera scanning the very building he now sits in. He toggles, zooming in on pod after colour-coded pod, and each occupant with a matching colour jacket, whispering, "Who are you...? Really."

And you...

And you....

***

Goodwin's gut is roiling. It's not because he witnesses the explosion and its bloody aftermath on repeat… the carnage. No. It's that his inner radar has hooked into something. A detail. But it has yet to rise into consciousness. Until then, he rewinds and rewinds, taking in the gore. The horror. He should take a break. A break may bring clarity. But no. Just one more rewind, then another and another until finally he's had enough. Gut-sick overrides the nagging radar. Wearily, he pushes away from the screen and heads for the beverage station.

He ponders an image now etched into his mind. The look on Yeorgi Stanovich's face just before he activated the detonator. It was like he was in pain. Not just psychic pain, but physical. Like a wounded animal.

In her interview, the ex-wife mentioned Stanovich had injured his leg when he leapt from her window to the sidewalk below. She saw him limp away. Had the wound been more than a sprain? Could that account for the excruciated look on his face just before the blast? A man on the run was unlikely to seek medical help. And seeing Bateman, he'd know The Beige was onto him. There was no escape. Too much going against him, too many points not in his favour, too much falling apart. No matter what, he was a dead man.

And so, the ultimate act.

It's at that second, as Goodwin leans against the cupboard with his steaming chicory, recalling the image of Stanovich sitting in his truck in pain, that the nagging detail flashes into awareness.

"That's it...."

A detail completely unrelated to an injury and pain. But it's the right detail because his gut stops roiling.

He sets down his mug and returns quickly to the monitor to view the cam footage again, taking it frame by frame, freezing on a single image: Bateman sitting on the bench under the tree. Stanovich in his truck. The unidentified man near the alley, pulling down his cap to obscure his face.

But there's something unobscured. Something both Stanovich and the unidentified man have in common. A detail so small and seemingly inconsequential, which he has viewed repeatedly without comprehending....

Neckerchiefs.

CHAPTER 11

In the beginning, the number of picketers was small. With their placards and banners held high, they were mostly silent, orderly. But covert rabble-rousers have inserted themselves into the crowd, intent on disrupting it. Now, after only two days, the protestors have transformed into a mob, their voices rising, becoming shrill, and angry…. *"Go back to where you came from!" "You're not one of us!" "You're robbing our children of their food…!"*

On and on it goes.

The mayor has summoned more of The Beige to quell the uprising. Still, someone flings a bottle, shattering it against the side of Marta and Sasha's container home.

Inside, Marta pulls Little Robert close. He's trembling.

"Why are they doing that, momma…?"

"They're angry."

"But what did we do wrong…?"

It's a tricky question. On the one hand, they've done nothing wrong. They simply sought refuge in a compound The Administration set up for them. But that's not the way the locals view it. To them, there's only so much food from the harvest to go around; only so much water from rivers and lakes which are drying up. If the village continues to grow, the locals fear none of them will survive.

It was clear to Marta that outsiders are unwelcome when the owner of the café refused her the server's job. Day after day the protest grows, leaving the refugees quivering inside their tin-can home, afraid to open the curtains in case someone should see them through a window and target them.

If The Beige cannot get the situation under control, there *will* be violence.

Sasha peeks out through a crack between the window curtains, seeing The Beige strong-arm the bottle-thrower away and heave him into the back of a van. Then they slap their batons against their palms to make it clear to the crowd that they will tolerate nothing out of bounds. They shift their gun belts, signalling that they will not hesitate.

The protestors settle. Raising their placards again, they march back and forth in front of the compound, their voices withering into resentful grumbling.

Sasha looks towards Marta, who strokes Little Robert's head to soothe him.

"We can't stay here…."

***

The Safehouse dominates a grassy hilltop. Yet it's somehow inconspicuous in its ordinariness: a low-slung ranch with petunias in hanging pots and a porch overlooking a winding river. It's been raining for three days. Sometimes a slow drizzle, at other times a deluge, transforming the once-lazy current into cresting waves.

Jack watches from a window as a fallen tree from somewhere upstream rides the rapids, rising and plunging like a white-water raft. If it snags under the nearby bridge, it could take it out, or it could block the flow, and the river will burst its banks. But it would take a catastrophic flood for the waters to reach the house atop the slope.

It was a miracle that the battery in the electric lasted long enough to get the three of them —Jack, Henry, and Elizabeth—across the plains to the foothills. And, thanks to the cryptic symbols on Henry's neckerchief, they had located the Safehouse just in time.

When the "host," an effeminate man fond of wearing tie-dyed caftans, saw them approach the porch, he had flung the door wide and greeted them with a hardy "Hello…!" He had met none of them before, but they were clearly recognizable from posters everywhere. Their undetected journey across the country astonished him. And even though there were no nearby neighbours to glimpse his guests, he had ushered them inside quickly, then removed a green blanket draped over the porch rail. For the past three days, he's fed them from his meagre stores and kept them warm and dry.

He told them how he'd followed the news closely. The Administration considers the Amphorium blast an act of terrorism. But others hail the group as heroes, signalling to those in charge that "voluntary" infusion is in fact extermination, and it's The Beige which deals in terror.

Both Jack and Henry could not help but reflect on the horror of Bateman and Goodwin dragging poor, terrified William away, and never seeing him again.

The host asked them if they had heard the news about Yeorgi Stanovich's suicide and about how Officer Bateman had died along with him. They had not. The gruesomeness of Bateman's death left both Jack and Henry agape and looking at one another in shocked disbelief.

Jack could have felt righteous satisfaction at Bateman's horrendous death, but he felt empty. Still, in his darker recesses, he wished it could've been him that took Bateman's life; *an eye for an eye....*

Elizabeth's heart sank at the news about Yeorgi, and she had shoved her plate aside. It was only after a long, thought-filled silence that she could finally speak.

"I'm not surprised...."

Lost in a mind's eye vision of the explosion,

Henry had shaken his head.

"Such a violent end…."

"He was so extreme. Destined to live a desperate life, no matter his options. He never stood a chance."

Henry was still shaking his head.

"But to take so many innocent lives. That was never the plan."

At that, Jack had abruptly pushed away from the table, scraping his chair across the floor. He stormed out of the room, calling out over his shoulder as he left, "What *was* the goddamn plan…?"

All of this had brought him to the window where he now stands watching the straggly roots of the fallen tree miss the underside of the bridge by inches, surging downstream towards another vulnerable bridge somewhere. Or to a bend in the river where it will snag, then converge with more flotsam, producing a dam.

There will be a flood.

For years now, the rain has never been where it's most needed; those parts of the country where it's parched, the earth cracked. And the sun never shines where it's most wanted, here and now, where hearts are low.

At least the rains have suppressed a massive forest fire in the nearby mountains. Elizabeth had said something cryptic about The Administration putting on a good show. But, thanks to the rain, the smoke from the fire no longer drifts across the foothills, fogging the view over the river. People can now step outside their homes without a sting in their throats and eyes.

Henry enters the room and leans against the doorjamb. He quietly watches Jack gazing out the window, then steps up behind him, wrapping his arms around his waist. He leans his chin on Jack's shoulder.

"I'm sorry...."

"For what?"

"For involving you in all this. I should've left you back there to disappear on your terms."

"I don't understand what we're doing, Henry. How you think we can win against The Administration?"

"I've told you. I refuse to die on their terms."

"But if they catch us...."

"Then it's over. But we *must* try."

He takes Jack's hand and leads him outside to the porch.

Still no sign of sun...

The sky hanging low...

Grim and dreary...

But the rain is only a drizzle now.

"Why blow up The Amphorium, Henry? That's not the act of the man I know; that I love."

"*Do* you still love me...?"

"I ran away, Henry. But I never stopped loving you."

Henry leans back against the porch rail.

"I blew up The Amphorium for the same

reason you ran away. I was hurting. The Administration took our William. I was angry that I wasn't there when they came; that you were alone. They hurt you, Jack, and you blamed yourself so badly that you ran away. They hurt you and they took our boy…."

There's a catch in his throat, and a tear streams down his cheek, and he sobs.

"They took our boy, Jack. I had to do something. I was so goddamn mad, so desperate, I lost my mind. I wanted to hurt them back…."

Jack reaches over and pulls Henry's head onto his shoulder. Until now, he has not realized just how pent-up Henry is. What he's held back; kept inside.

"Shhh…."

He kisses the top of Henry's head. He's never known him to cry this way. Usually, he's the stoic one; the strong one.

Jack embraces him until, in time, Henry cries himself out and breathes a heavy sigh. It's a release he's needed for a long time.

"I've gotten us in so deep, Jack. I'm sorry…."

Jack loosens the knot on Henry's neckerchief and dabs at the tears as he repeats a phrase from what seems like a long time ago…

"The answer to the question, 'To be, or not to be?' is *always* 'To be….'"

"I keep telling you The Haven exists, Jack. And I've promised I'll get us there if it's my last act."

"That statement's too ominous, my love. Take it back. It'll not be your last act."

Henry offers a weak smile.

"I take it back…."

He turns and gazes out over the river. It still rages.

"Who knew that getting old would bring emotions so close to the surface? We're supposed to be wise, Jack. Instead, I feel so vulnerable. So easily hurt."

As Jack watches him, he reflects on their lives together. How the two of them have loved one another from the minute they met as young boys, and all the way to this moment; two men standing on a porch on a dreary day when the world around them is falling apart, and they're hunted. But with the promise of a better place somewhere down the road.

Again, Henry steps up behind Jack and wraps his arms around his waist and pulls him close. He's always done it this way. Jack leans back into Henry's chest. Like always, he feels safe. And, for now, he believes the promise.

***

Little Robert cannot keep his eyes open. His head bobs as Sasha carries him through inky darkness to the truck. It's the middle of the night and Little Robert was in a deep sleep.

Marta has gathered food, along with the meagre possessions they gathered after moving into the container home and stuffed all of it into a single box. She'll drive the truck while Sasha cradles Little Robert, hoping to keep him calm while they make their escape.

For a week, the protestors have arrived early each morning brandishing their placards and shouting until sundown. So far, their actions have failed to move the mayor from his support for the refugees, even though he knows it's likely to mean a loss in the next election. Over time, the words on the placards have become more vitriolic... *"You should have burned with the town you came from...."*

More bottles tossed...

Paint bombs.

Each time the level of vandalism rises, The Beige become harsher. They beat the aggressors, bloody, with their clubs before wrestling them into a van. This only intensifies the rising tension.

When rocks shatter a window on Marta and Sasha's container home, and that of a neighbour, they decide it's time to leave.

The Administration has imposed a curfew on the protestors, forcing them to return to their homes by sundown each day. And throughout the night, The Beige makes random patrols of the compound to safeguard peace for the residents. Anyone found out after dark faces incarceration. Or worse.

Switching off a lamp, Sasha watches through a crack in the curtain as the most recent patrol finishes a slow drive-by and circles back towards the village, headlights disappearing into the night.

Now is the time to get out.

Their future destination is uncertain. Sasha knows of a great uncle far from Coal Town. They've never been close, and Sasha barely knows him. But the great uncle is aging into Eveningsong, and Sasha can only hope that he'll be sympathetic to them. After involving himself in the bomb plot, he knows he can never see his immediate family ever again… if he survives. And although there's a chance The Administration might track a distant relative, the great uncle is their only option. But Sasha tells Marta that, no matter what, they'll keep going—together—until they find a place to land.

As Marta sets the box into the back of the truck, Sasha slips inside holding Little Robert, who immediately falls back into a deep sleep. Marta climbs behind the steering wheel, closing the truck door carefully. It makes only a soft click. It's crucial that they not wake neighbours made jittery from protests. Pressing the ignition button, the electric hums with only a soft purr. Gravel crackles under tires as they roll over the road leading off the compound to the highway.

Once out of the gate, Marta turns westward and speeds up.

Immediately, headlights pierce the rear window and red and blue lights flash. The patrol car has circled back again.

Marta startles, and a shock rockets through

Sasha's chest. He looks towards Marta, who looks back at him, panicked.

"Should I gun it…?"

To Sasha, eternity compacts into a split second as he envisions what a high-speed chase would look like, and its probable outcome. His shoulders slump, and his face sags into resignation. He shakes his head.

"No. We'd endanger Little Robert…."

The lights continue to flash as the patrol car follows them closely. A woman's voice blasts through a speaker, authoritatively. "Pull over. Now…."

Marta steers the truck to the side of the road, glancing at Sasha.

Desperation…

Suffocating dread.

Little Robert rouses, rubbing his eyes. "Momma…?"

Marta grips the steering wheel, her knuckles white as she watches through the side mirror, seeing one of The Beige, who steps out of the patrol car and approaches with caution; one hand holding a flashlight and the other balanced on a gun holster.

Rigid, Sasha stares straight ahead and into the darkness, wishing it would swallow him up; make him disappear. He's made it farther than he ever thought he might. But now it's the end.

A trial…

Infusion…

Death.

He gives a quick look at the side-view mirror, seeing another officer step from the passenger side of the patrol car. The silhouette of a woman against the glare of the headlights. She stands near the front of the vehicle, a hand also near her gun holster.

A vision flashes through Sasha's mind.

Him bolting across the field into darkness.

Tall grass whipping at his ankles.

But then gunfire...

The impact of a bullet in his back...

Falling...

Little Robert's horror at the sight.

He sends up a soft prayer that when The Beige takes him, their reputation aside, they'll show restraint and compassion towards Marta and Little Robert.

Marta winds down the window as the officer approaches. It's Ginni.

She shines her flashlight into the cab, blinding Marta as she barks.

"Where you folks headed this time of night...?"

She sweeps her beam of light throughout the cab, first landing on Little Robert, who squints and shields his eyes from the glare. Then to Sasha's profile, as he stares straight ahead.

After long thought-filled seconds, he turns, looking directly at Ginni, fixedly. No hint of challenge or defiance. As if saying, *"Yes, it's me,*

Sasha Dobrev...."

Ginni startles...

Recognition...

Stunned silence.

But then Marta interjects. "We don't feel safe here anymore. We're going to live with family far west and we're just getting an early start, that's all."

Ginni's eyes narrow as she continues to take in Sasha: his closely cropped hair, the familiar eyes, the distinctive nose from the image she has seen on posters everywhere.

Out of the darkness, Lila's voice.

"Everything alright, officer...?"

Ginni holds up a hand to her, flat palmed.

She refocuses her flashlight on Little Robert, who looks back at her, bewildered.

"Is this your daddy, boy...?"

Little Robert looks up at Sasha, then back into the light, squinting. He presses himself into Sasha's chest.

"I'm *Little* Robert. He's *Big* Robert...."

Ginni's mouth puckers as she takes in the boy and his innocent return gaze, then to Sasha again.

He looks back at her, unwavering, waiting; the man who blew up The Amphorium. Someone associated with Yeorgi Stanovich, the man who incinerated her former lover. Here, in a truck in the middle of the night, outside a village in the far country.

Sasha Dobrev, she's certain of it. Alias Big Robert.

And a woman…

And a frightened child.

From the darkness, Lila's voice again.

"Officer…?"

"Yes, yes…."

Returning her attention to Marta, she breathes in a long breath and lets it out, overwhelmed, conflicted.

Then, as though standing outside herself, she hears her own voice, strangely detached, speaking words which, as an officer of The Beige, are the wrong words, but which come from a deep, heartfelt place…

"It's a dark night…. Safe trip."

Marta looks back at her, disbelieving, uncertain.

Ginni jolts her head toward the highway.

The look of worry on Marta's face melts into a grateful but cautious smile. She nods and steers back onto the road and away.

As Lila climbs back into the patrol car, she calls out to Ginni, who has not moved.

"Coming…?"

"Yes. Yes…."

Silhouetted against the headlights of the patrol car, Ginni watches as Marta's truck disappears over the crest of a hill.

***

Elizabeth's eyelids riffle as she dreams about her father. It's as though he's standing right there, next to her mattress, prodding her to waken. She expects to see him when she opens her eyes, but no. Only the darkness in a windowless room in the Safehouse; a hidden place where others before her have secreted themselves while making their escape. The entrance to the room is through an unobtrusive sliding panel behind a bookcase attached to the wall on a squeaky hinge. When Elizabeth first saw it, she thought about *'The Diary of Anne Frank.'* There are two small vents creating a gentle draft, so the air is not completely still, and a faint nightlight illuminates the way to a cramped closet with a toilet and sink. Elizabeth had felt uneasy when she first entered the secret room. There's only one way in and, therefore, one way out. If The Beige ever discovers it, there's no escape.

Dreaming about her father is not coincidental. Not just because she dreams about him often, but because she's now so close to The Haven. It really exists. It's just that, according to her father, it's not exactly where The Administration wants people to believe it is. Nor is it *what* people believe it to be. This is what she must prove; what her father had wanted to prove before The Beige shot him dead. Not only because he wanted to warn the people. But also to expose the truth to them. And even though it'll lead to anarchy again, ordinary citizens have a right to know.

She peers through the dimness at Henry and Jack, curled up and asleep next to each other on another mattress. It was Henry who brought her together with Yeorgi and Sasha. He's a sharp-eyed man who, from his desk at the library, put pieces together. Within three disparate people, he detected cohesion even though, at first, none of them were aware of each other. He recognized his own anguish. His anger. His hatred of The Administration.

He saw how Elizabeth, Sasha, and Yeorgi all avoided technology while researching at his out-of-the-way branch. Instead, they relied on hard copy books only, which they never signed out, and from which they only took notes, each aiming to remain untraceable. But, Henry, surreptitiously surveying the subjects they studied: for Elizabeth, complex coding, for Sasha, revolutions throughout history, for Yeorgi, explosives, and detonation in the mining industry—sensed that each was a radical in the making. Each had the same goal—his goal—disruption of The Administration.

When the hinge on the bookcase squeaks, Elizabeth, Jack, and Henry sit bolt upright on their mattresses, waiting, wondering. Is it the host? Or is The Beige making a raid? The room floods with sudden blinding light.

The host peers in, chiming, "Acorns are

brewing...."

Relief.

The host has robbed his hens of a half-dozen precious eggs, which he scrambles. He fries up hash browns using potatoes harvested from his back garden along with tomatoes, which he sautés in oleo. Real butter is scarce.

Henry savours a sip of hot faux coffee.

"I can't tell you how grateful we are."

The host slides tomatoes onto Henry's plate.

"We've got to stick together. If things don't change, infusion is only a year off for me, too."

Just like so many others who have helped the group along the way, he has nothing to lose. Whether he ages into Eveningsong, or The Administration catches him aiding the rebels, the outcome is the same. Infusion. Hope only lays in Jack and Henry escaping. If they can do it, then others can. To the host's way of thinking, overpopulation is a problem, but more so is the corrupt and greedy elite—and make no mistake, an elite still exists—who continue to make a fortune while destroying the ecological balance. Only rebellion will force The Administration to change. But, for now, he must shift the angry sermon in his head. If he doesn't, he'll spiral into angry darkness. And he doesn't want that. Not today.

He tells Henry that, thanks to The Fringe, he's scared up another electric for him and Jack.

"It's battered and decrepit, but it'll get you to

the next Safehouse."

It's only then that Jack realizes that he and Henry will travel separately from Elizabeth. He remembers the rule about travelling apart for safety. But when Henry speaks again, it's clear that there are other reasons.

"I hope you find what you're looking for, Elizabeth; prove your father right and get the message out...."

Elizabeth reaches into the pocket of her cardigan, taking out a smartphone. She waves it at Henry and winks.

Jack's eyes dart back and forth between the two of them. Henry's statement confuses him, and Elizabeth's phone has surprised him. As far as he's aware, the group had given up all their technology when they fled, so that The Administration couldn't track them. But here is Elizabeth, holding up a smartphone. It could be just a burner. If she ever powers up, she's doomed.

From the outset, Henry has held back and kept so much information to himself. Is Elizabeth not heading to The Haven like they are? What is she "looking for"? And what "message" must she get out? He knows that, even if he asks, Henry won't tell him. He'll only say that it's best that no one knows the complete story in case The Administration captures any of them. Still, Jack suspects if anyone knows the entire story, it's Henry.

They wait until well after sundown before

leaving the Safehouse in their separate cars. And just as he had done with the farmer and his family, Jack watches through the rear window as the ranch house and the host diminish into nothingness. And just as with the farmer and his family, the host remains nameless.

For a while, with Henry at the wheel, they follow Elizabeth's car along the same route, until arriving at a fork in the road. Both vehicles pull over and they all get out. Henry embraces Elizabeth.

"I hope your plan works out, Elizabeth."

"With luck...."

Again, Jack is confused. What plan...?

Elizabeth reaches out, embracing Jack, long and hard.

"Take care of your man...."

With this, she returns to her electric and steers it onto the southwest fork. Jack and Henry watch as Elizabeth's taillights disappear into the night, both sensing in the pits of their stomachs that they will never see her again.

They return to their electric, and Henry steers onto the northwest fork. The road through the foothills is dark. The distant mountains loom like black paper cutouts against a deep blue sky. But the closer they get, the more three dimensional they become. With moonlight reflecting off their faceted surfaces, the mountains embrace all sides of a narrow, abandoned logging road, leading deeper into solitude.

From her car, Elizabeth looks out at the same mountains.

Dark...

Forbidding...

The road ahead, lonely...

No surreptitious fellow escapees travelling to The Haven by night, and Elizabeth knows why.

The fighter jets she had witnessed streaking across the sky over the prairie farm had strategically bombed an area in the mountains where people believe The Haven to be. The Administration's propaganda machine immediately churned out stories about the destruction of the entire area. Therefore, it's now a fruitless pursuit for anyone attempting to escape Eveningsong. There's no place for them to go. People had seen for themselves the smoke from the ensuing forest fire rise out of the mountains and drift east across the entire country.

Elizabeth will not waste time seeking the site. She suspects there's only burned-out forest there, anyway. No destroyed structures. No charred bodies. The Administration will put on a good show and secure the area with armed Beige. But a clean-up operation is unnecessary.

The second site is the important one; the real Haven, hidden and almost inaccessible unless one knows where to look. Thanks to her father, Elizabeth knows.

In the meantime, she'll seek the last Safehouse. She reaches into the pocket of her cardigan, looking for the neckerchief map she had balled up and stowed away. But it's not there. She pulls the car over to the side of the road, and in the dim light, she checks all her pockets. She combs through the entire vehicle, checking under seats and floor mats.

The map is nowhere.

CHAPTER 12

The farmer's son hands over Elizabeth's neckerchief to Alistair Goodwin. He'd unearthed it amongst the rubble of the farmhouse after she and the others left. He doesn't understand its meaning, but he suspects it's significant because he saw Henry consult another just like it before leaving.

Still stinging from the loss of everything to the windstorm, and still outraged that his parents aided the rebellion, he'd contacted The Administration.

It's his duty.

Goodwin accepts the neckerchief with a mixture of gratitude and abhorrence. Gratitude, because it may lead him to the rebels. Abhorrence because the farmer's son naively betrayed his own parents, believing what The Administration has drummed into him from an early age.

Duty.

But also, trusting that by cooperating, The Beige will spare his parents. A belief, now shattered as he witnesses them dragged away. He's naïve, and he trusts the ideology, so how could he know The Administration spares no one for the sake of duty?

There, amid the devastation of the family farm, the farmer's son falls to his knees, weeping, pleading...

"But I cooperated...."

He reaches out to his father and mother as The Beige push them into the back of a van.

"I cooperated...."

One last glimpse of his father's sorrowful face, robbed of twenty more years before his natural Eveningsong.

After this, one of two things will happen. Through his sobbing, the farmer's son will rationalize that, his loss aside, it was the right thing to do for the sake of the cause. Or, more likely, he'll become a rebel in-waiting. The Administration counts on people believing its deeply imbedded doctrine of saving the planet through infusion, but the mere existence of The Group-of-Five belies the notion.

One of The Beige goes to the young man and raises him to his feet, still sobbing.

"You did the right thing...."

He leads him away. The Administration will give him a home somewhere. And, without a doubt, a job, on this same farm, which they will seize for the state.

Later, when everyone is gone, and Goodwin is alone, he looks around at the ravaged landscape.

He can't help but feel awed by the power of nature. And tormented when he remembers his own losses at its hand: Melinda, Nicholas.

Now this.

A toppled barn...

A shattered house...

Heavy machinery scattered over prairie land like toys across a playroom floor...

Losing the farm now part of history, if there is ever a future generation to trace the family tree.

The nearby town is in ruins. The Administration has disaster relief programs, but there are so many climate catastrophes nowadays, it's difficult to keep up. It'll be a long time before proper aid arrives.

Goodwin breathes in deeply, sniffing the air. It *is* sweeter, isn't it?

Isn't it...?

He sinks to his knees and then lays, prostrate, on the ground. He breathes in the soil's smell. The power of nature will bring it all back. Surely. Repair the ruin. Yes...! See there. A horde of ants, tunnelling, toiling, spreading out across the land; lifting and carrying fifty times their weight. If the wind swept them away, they've returned. He rolls onto his back. Let the ants carry him away if they will.

Laying there, taking in the sky's vastness, he wants to believe that it's not too late; that nature has not passed the tipping point. But at the horizon, there's a thin ring of brown, smudging into the blue. Why is there still smog after everything they've done to prevent it?

He thinks about the hundreds of abandoned, dried-up oil wells spread across the prairie, for which no one, including his former employers, takes responsibility. And the others that continue to pump.

The world hasn't acted fast enough…

Instead, now reacting in a panic…

Becoming uncivil for the sake of saving civilization.

And him, a part of it; tracking those who are nonconforming. He thinks about all the things he's done; the operations he's conducted on behalf of The Administration. He thinks about what he must do when he finds the rebels: Henry and Jack. He cringes at the memory of William; his part in it, and springs back up and onto his feet…

"Change the thought process… Change it."

Taking out the neckerchief, he holds it up to the sunlight, spread wide. Its cryptic symbols will be telling. He's convinced it's a code. While reviewing the footage of the suicide bombing, he saw that Yeorgi and the man he suspects is Sasha Dobrev each wore them. And he took a second look at the footage of The Group-of-Five gathered at The Amphorium for the funeral of Yelena Chomsky. All but Jack Parnell wore an identical neckerchief. Maybe Parnell didn't need one because his husband has one. The only other oddity is that Elizabeth Lowell wore hers wrapped around her wrist, like a bracelet. Undoubtedly, a fashion choice and therefore, insignificant.

Looking at the neckerchief, he can, even now, detect patterns within the pattern. He'll scan it and run it through AI, which will decipher the code within minutes. Unless Elizabeth Lowell has compromised even it.

So far, the rebels have used the crudest methods to evade capture. And they've sabotaged the technology upon which The Administration relies.

It's laughable.

***

The Senior…

Alone in his office…

Studying the monitors.

Besides the usual sordid stuff which he observes day-to-day, an on-site camera shows a research team floating offshore in the Atlantic, testing for salinity and temperature. Internal reports outline how oceans continue to warm, and more species of fish are dying off. In real time, another monitor shows a dry riverbed, and another a shrinking lake. Yet another shows floodwater rushing through the streets of an Italian village, taking citizens, livestock, and ancient structures with it. The Senior mumbles to himself, *"Poor bastards…."*

Icecaps continue to melt, causing fissures to snake through rock faces, making them unstable.

Yet, using external reports, The Administration assures people that there are signs of renewal. The air is sweeter, with fewer particulates, even though it seems thinner and hotter; even though the people witness with their own eyes, plants dry out and wilt, they choose to believe.

Fires erupt, consuming forests...

One natural system fails, and then the next, and the next...

Monitor after monitor. It's disheartening.

Still, The Administration releases reassuring reports to the public, as captains of industry continue to push the limit.

The Senior, scanning his monitors, fears the limit is past.

His eye catches a particular monitor. On the other side of the world, a minor rebellion has broken out, which The Administration there is finding difficult to suppress. Protestors outnumber The Beige, and The Senior can't help but wonder if it's a sign of things to come. For a good decade, the New Order has kept things under control. But now, systems are becoming ragged, unravelling.

Closer to home, Coal Town is a prime example. Things there are heating up. So far, the mayor has been ineffectual, and The Senior wonders if he's still on the side of The Administration. Complaints about more climate refugees grow by the day. People act out of fear. There's also a counter protest from those who welcome the refugees and encourage compassion and tolerance. And, just like the rebellion on the other side of the world, militants, both pro and con, soon outnumber The Beige.

Another monitor displays the site of the Amphorium bombing. The Administration still has the area cordoned off. Protesters and counter protesters gather there. Lately, a movement sympathetic to the rebels has emerged from the shadows. The Senior can't decide if they're incredibly brave or incredibly reckless. Revealing themselves publicly as part of The Fringe exposes them to a treason charge, and they're in danger of infusion. The only reason The Administration has restrained themselves is because they don't want to martyr them and show that infusion is extermination.

Besides, others who believe in the doctrine, turn out in numbers to shout them down.

Every once-in-a-while someone from either side bursts the line and attacks. The Beige take immediate action, dragging away the offender. Rumours run rampant that The Administration infuses such delinquents, no matter which side they're on. The Senior knows that's untrue. The Beige only return them to their homes, albeit with bruises and lacerations which were not there before, warning them to cease and desist. Still, the rumours of infusion persist, which only intensifies hostility towards The Administration.

The more The Senior studies the situation,

it's apparent that the partisan divide is widening. Worse still, all sides have lost sight of what exactly they're fighting for or against, and their overnuanced beliefs have muddied. Suppressed anger is palpable, threatening to burst at the seams.

He thinks to himself, *"God forbid they find out the true nature of The Haven. They'll riot in the streets...."*

The Senior watches on the monitor as The Beige struggle with two miscreants, one from each side, and tosses them into the back of the same van. He questions if, once the van arrives at its destination and they unlock it, they'll discover one, or even two dead bodies, each having fought the other to the death. And although it's not the prescribed procedure, he wonders if that's the plan all along.

***

Ta-tum, ta-tum, ta-tum…

The beat of a snare drum. It unifies the crowd behind a single purpose, a common belief.

Brrrr-um-tum, ta-tum…

Constant. Unvaried. Ta-tum….

Fury churns in a young man's gut like a raging sea. Scorching bile rises into his throat, and he spits out words more bitter than those scrawled on his placard…

"Get the fuck out of our town…."

Tatum.

But screeching is not enough. A placard is

not enough. He scans the line of Beige with their protective shields, batons, and sidearms. Holding strong, they form a barrier in front of the refugee compound. Among them are Lila and Ginni, there to maintain order at the shrillest protest yet.

Driven to act, the young man picks up a stone and pitches it, hard. It glances off Lila's helmet. At first the crowd falls silent, dumbfounded. Then it surges forward with a roar. Immediately, The Beige advance en mass, banging their shields with their batons. The sound overpowers the beat of the drum.

Frightened, the mob retreats.

Having felt the impact of the stone, Lila whips out her pistol …

Where in the hell did that come from…?

She scans the crowd with a venomous glare. Each pair of eyes in the crowd is blank, un-telling. But, in an instant, she catches it. A young woman's subconscious sideways glance betrays the young man standing next to her. Out of instinct, Lila turns her pistol on him. The young man stares back at her, wide-eyed, fearful. She envisions a bullet streaking towards him, blowing a bloody hole in his chest…

"STOP…!"

A man's voice…

Strong…

Authoritative…

Cutting through the din, freezing everyone in place.

In the commotion, no one noticed the mayor arrive at the scene. He has stepped out of a polished black electric. His assistant stands nearby with a hand still on the door handle. Taking it all in, the mayor threads his way through the crowd, placing himself between the protestors and the line of Beige.

Again, his voice...

Sharp...

Commanding.

"Let me be clear. There will be no violence today."

Lila has not moved. She still has her gun trained on the young man. But Ginni steps up beside her, pushing her arm down, pointing the pistol at the ground. Lila blinks, as if emerging from a trance. She gazes down at the pistol, then back up at the young man, shocked that she had come so close to shooting him. She pictures him falling to the ground, dead. The crowd rampaging, overwhelming The Beige.

Another voice rises out of the crowd...

"We want the bastards out...."

The mayor raises his hand as if to block the offensive words in mid-air.

"Let me be clear again. No one is going anywhere."

Yet another voice from the crowd...

"There's more of us than there are of you."

Chants from the mob...

Fists punch the air...

The placards wave…

Ta-tum, ta-tum.

A forceful presence, the mayor still has his hand raised, flat. There's something in his steady manner that grips the crowd; quells them. Maybe they're still unused to bucking authority. Maybe out of respect for the mayor at this moment, they remember he recently lost his only son. He motions towards the compound.

"You will do nothing to harm these people."

The voice of the angry young man again…

"One of them could be another bomber. You never know."

Off to the side, Ginni flinches, remembering the night she came face to face with Sasha Dobrev on the road outside the compound.

The mayor curls his fingers, beckoning the young man.

"Come here, son."

The young man looks side to side. With his chin jutting out, he steps up to the mayor, defiant. Instinctively, the crowd forms an arc around them, ready to take in the words. Alerted, The Beige tense. But the mayor turns to them…

"Be calm. Everyone…."

He sizes up the young man.

"You're just a child."

The young man puffs out his chest.

"I'm seventeen."

"My son's age…."

Looking at the mayor, the young man

glimpses a great sadness flooding his eyes, and his puffed-out chest deflates. His glare softens.

"I knew him at school...."

The mayor places his hand on the young man's shoulder.

"He died because he disagreed with The Administration's policy on infusion. You appear ready to die while harming the people he would save."

He tilts his head towards the compound.

"They're human souls, you know, just like you. They live. They breathe. They hope. They dream. And they have a right to be here, just as you do."

"But there's not enough to go around. The crops are failing."

"Then plant again. Even if it's just one seed. Then nurture it."

The young man snorts.

"One seed...."

"There's hope in a seed. But in what you're doing..."

The mayor bends down and picks up the stone the young man hurled.

"...there's only destruction. Death. Don't you see...?"

He looks at the mob, taking in each person. He knows most by name.

"Harley, you know better than to be here. And Edwina...."

A man and a woman in the crowd lower

their eyes.

"We *must* find a way, all of us. Even in these perilous times, we *must* take care of each other. If we don't, then… well, nobody wins."

Winding back through the crowd, he walks towards his car.

"Go home, everyone. Go home."

Later that evening, he sits alone in his den, sipping scotch and thinking about his wife, who still suffers from the loss of her son. Sometimes, in the middle of the night, she wakens, wailing. He embraces her until she cries herself dry and falls back into an exhausted sleep. Through shared suffering, he's grown to love her more deeply. And finding strength, he never knew he had. He's been her rock.

He takes another sip of scotch. No one's more surprised than he that he could summon the courage to confront the mob today. He thinks about the angry young man and all others like him. They see no future. That's why they're willing to go to extremes, threatening the lives of others. Worse still, blowing up an Amphorium like The Group-of-Five did; setting off a chain of events which has threatened civility everywhere; a ripple effect like that which continues to endanger the world's ecology. A ripple effect that swept up his son.

Tilting the glass and swallowing the last drop of scotch, he questions whether he himself believes the philosophy he spouted at the young man today; whether there's hope in a single seed.

Yes.

He resolves that tomorrow he'll plant something and nurture it; give all his hope to it. And he'll do what he can to inspire hope and strength and courage in the villagers too.

Glancing at the half-empty bottle of scotch sitting on his desk, he wonders if that's where he's found his sudden courage. And if he'll feel the same way tomorrow.

No matter.

For now, he'll climb the stair, slip under the green velvet coverlet, and embrace his grieving wife. He'll pull her close and soothe her tortured soul.

***

"God help me if I'd pulled the trigger...."

Lila's hand trembles as she takes a sip of beer. She and Ginni sit together in the pub, commiserating over the day's events.

"I don't know what happened, but when that rock hit my helmet...."

Her words melt away as she stares into space, reimagining a scene, which, thankfully, never happened. A bullet piercing the young man's chest. Just a boy, really.

"Don't beat yourself up."

Ginni's consoling words bring Lila back.

"But we're trained to remain cool in situations like that."

It's true. The Beige's rigorous training weeds out those who cannot withstand the pressure, especially considering the recent loss of a team member in the explosion. But it's more than that. It feels like something has come loose; a new line crossed. For whatever reason, people are losing their sense of shared purpose.

The two women sit silently, lost in their own thoughts. Lila, replaying the scene at the protest over and over and thanking God that the mayor stepped in when he did; Ginni, wrapped up in remembrance of the night she came face to face with the terrorist, Sasha Dobrev.

The angry young man at the protests was right. There *was* a bomber living amongst the refugees. And she'd let him go. Just as Lila had forgotten her training under pressure, Ginni had abandoned her oath to The Administration.

Why...?

The remembrance is clear: she, commanding the driver of a truck to pull over to the side of the road outside the compound. Shining her flashlight into the cab and seeing Dobrev. Certain it was him. And just like Lila today, instinctively reaching for her pistol.

But there was something in Sasha Dobrev's return gaze. There was no fight left in him. Instead, he had the look of a man caught up in something well beyond what he intended, now ready to concede and accept the only probable outcome. Infusion.

Hope lost.

But there was also something in the way he so gently cradled the boy; a boy innocent of everything and feeling safe in the arms of a man he calls Big Robert. And there was something in the way the woman with Dobrev had looked at her, clearly envisioning a scenario where she too was about to lose everything: her son, this man, even her own life. Which is certain given the current regime.

In that instant, despite Dobrev's involvement in the destruction of The Amphorium, it felt right to let all of them go.

She thinks about the mayor's speech today, offering hope to people living on a dying planet. Hope when they have no life beyond a specified date, their Eveningsong. Hope that comes with planting a single seed. Not for oneself. But for a future generation that may never actualize in an unclear future.

Only now is she coming to realize how deeply the speech resonated with her.

Sitting there in the pub with Lila, someone who lost her composure because she too has lost hope, Ginni tells herself that hope is what she gave Dobrev on that dark night at the side of the road. Hope. And to the woman and the boy who calls himself Little Robert.

***

In an instant, AI broke the code and created

a map. Goodwin has the encoded neckerchief spread out before him on a table. And next to it a sheet of paper with a complete diagram outlining the location of all Safehouses across the country, coast to coast. Even the ones The Administration has already discovered for themselves and bulldozed. He's certain the map is accurate because it shows the devastated farm where three of The Group-of-Five: Elizabeth Lowell, Henry Chagall and Jack Parnell passed through, proving what he has suspected all along. They're travelling west. If he shares the encoded map with The Administration, the entire underground will cease to exist.

What intrigues him most about the map is the second to last location, 'The Haven.' There are clear directions to a site deep in the western mountains. Thinking back to the firebombing of the administration building, he recalls the last conversation he had with The Senior before leaving the city:

Him: "...I suspect The Group-of-Five is heading west. Possibly to The Haven."

The Senior: "It doesn't exist, poor fools...."

Yet, here it is, on the neckerchief map, which has proven accurate in all other respects. He cannot understand The Senior and The Administration not knowing the exact location of such a place. They have satellite imagery. But, then again, they've not known the location of all the Safehouses, until now. But The Senior was emphatic, The Haven doesn't exist; even entirely denying a faint possibility.

Goodwin is aware of myths about the place that people latch onto... an Eden. Or fears that The Haven is a trap which The Administration sets as a way of ensnaring and bringing back anyone who sets out to find it. But, thinking back, he can't recall a time when The Administration has ever brought anyone back. Certainly, they have publicized no captures, which is something they'd do to continue asserting their authority. He's beginning to believe that a haven really exists, and people have successfully escaped to it.

CHAPTER 13

Imposing rock cliffs, looming...

An isolated valley...

Water rushing over stones in a stream running into a crystalline lake ...

Hissing breeze through swaying pines...

A lone cabin...

Except for solar panels on the rooftop, all of it is like something out of the past, as though stepping into pioneer days...

Peace...

Solitude.

Sitting alone in a rustic chair on the porch, a familiar woman, dressed in blue jeans and a denim shirt: Yelena Chomsky. After faking her own Eveningsong—the rebellious are everywhere, even inside an Amphorium—she made her way across the country to this secluded place. The Administration did not think to seek her out or track her. They believed she was dead. Just another data point in the bank of the infused. So, unchallenged, she arrived at this idyllic place.

And now she waits.

Leaning back in the chair, she gazes out over the sun-dappled lake. Even though everywhere there is serenity, her eyes betray silent concern. She's been alone for weeks now, and she wonders if aloneness is her future. The others have yet to arrive, and since there's no communication with the outside world, she's uncertain if they ever will. Did they fail in their attempt to escape? The Administration may have captured them. Infused them. Each day, she awakens with expectation. Today will be the day they emerge from the bush. She wishes it into existence. But until then, her only company: a lone black bear roaming the forest, deer, cougars, and the wolves which are a constant threat to her chickens and goats. That any of these breeds have yet to die off completely offers hope for her own continued survival, and for that of the others. If they ever come.

God help her if The Beige crash through the bush with their pistols at the ready, having used satellite imagery or drones to zero in on her unlawful refuge. But be it a raging beast or human foe, she has a rifle always at the ready. Even now, it leans against the porch rail.

Rising from the chair, she carries a tin bucket to the rushing stream. She fills it to the brim and lugs it, splish-splashing, back to a garden patch, where she pours water between rows of potatoes, onions, carrots, tomatoes, and corn. It'll be weeks before any of it's ready to harvest. Until then, there should be enough stores to feed her and the others. Yes, she must keep believing there *will* be others.

Over a year ago, she and Henry Chagall had made their way back and forth across the country preparing this place; preparing for the day they made their escape. Beyond their impending Eveningsong, each has sensed the country, if not the world, will descend into war. It's bound to. For so many reasons: partisan politics, religious sectarianism, hatred of The Administration, and fears around an increasingly hostile climate, tensions have reached a boiling point. Like a volcano building up enormous energy, there can be only one outcome. Eruption.

After William's infusion, guilt and grief racked Henry and Jack until, finally, Jack left. It was then that Yelena and Henry began forming their plan. The Administration, with its law of Each-One-for-Everyone, be damned. Both are determined to die on their terms. Working on and off, it took them over a year to build this quiet place, this Eden in the middle of nowhere.

But, over that year, Yelena noticed a change in Henry. The man, who at first wanted only to save himself, became someone more radical; someone who not only wanted to escape The Administration but to do damage to it on his way out the door. It worried Yelena that he had connected himself to the militants and indeed formed his own cell of like-minded people.

She agreed with Henry's desire to seek Jack and to plead with him to come to the cabin. She wants him there too. But she begged Henry not to go through with the bombing plot; to risk drawing attention to himself, and therefore to her. He was resolute.

On the day of her faked infusion, the sight of Jack sitting next to Henry in The Amphorium overjoyed her. It meant there was hope for them as a pair. But the look in Henry's eyes alarmed her. She knew he had decided. He and his cohorts would set the bomb.

So, now she sits alone on the porch, peering into the forest, wondering if Henry, Jack, or any of the others will ever make their way along a hidden path. And even if they arrive here, she wonders if all of them can endure this place. It's one thing to study books about survivalism and living off-grid. It's another to attempt it. Others have tried and failed because of ill-preparation; later found dead from starvation or exposure. And the isolation has driven more than one to madness. Yelena will risk it. She, like the others, wants to die on her terms.

Night after night, though, she lays in the dark, listening to the rustle of nocturnal animals skulking outside the cabin. And she hears them skitter away when solar lamps snap on after sensing their approach. Also, a high-pitched electronic whistle to frighten them. It happens repeatedly throughout the night. And as she lays there, she wonders what it'll be like if none of the others arrive. Will she go mad? Illness or injury might take her. It could be nature itself: forest fire, blizzard, or flash flood like the one two days ago. The rain had come in a torrent, transforming the rushing creek flowing in and out of the lake into a raging river that threatened the garden and the cabin. The cliffs at the north end of the valley turned into Niagara, with water coursing over its cragged rock face and through its crevices, making it unstable.

Or the wolves may get all her goats and chickens. She'll become malnourished from a lack of milk, cheese, and eggs. In the dark, she understands why superstitious ancient peoples manifested fairies and goblins to explain bumps in the night. Even Gods to pray to. Often, she switches on a solar lamp, shining a light into all corners of the cabin, then prays for dawn.

Now here, on the porch, alone, she hears a sudden rustling in the bush. Trembling, she aims the rifle at the woods, only to lower it again. Tears flood her eyes when two bedraggled and half-starved figures stumble into the clearing. Jack and Henry have arrived....

***

"Dadda... Daddaaaa...."

Alistair Goodwin, trapped in a dream again.

William, the man-child, lies on a table looking lost and confused. He doesn't know why he's there. Even in the dream, Goodwin can't stomach his innocent questioning.

"Dadda... where's Dadda...?"

Goodwin struggles to run towards him, but his feet are in sludge. The harder he strains, the stiffer his legs feel...

And the man-child, his arm exposed...

An attendant inserts an infusion hose...

The needle pricks William...

Softly... "Ow...."

The attendant...

"Shh, William... shh. It's sleep time now."

A feeble attempt to make the whimpering man-child understand.

"Dadda...."

In the real world, Goodwin twitches in bed. Beads of sweat bubble on his brow.

Then, back in the dream...

William seems to get farther away from Goodwin as he struggles to reach him.

His feet, heavy as bricks...

Stuck in the mire...

William drifts...

His whisper becomes a sob...

"Daddaaa...."

Drifting...

Drifting...

Now in a deep sleep...

Goodwin, reaching out...

Straining...

The blips on the heart monitor slowing, slowing....

Straining...
Stop.

Goodwin awakens suddenly to an unfamiliar room; no recognizable signs to ground him; bring him back: the desk, the chair, the collection of framed butterflies he bought to commemorate his boy. None of it.

He tosses aside the sodden blankets and stumbles to his feet, thinking, *"Where in hell's the bathroom in this god-awful place...?"* Finally, icy water on his face, now dripping. Gasping, he peers into the mirror, uncertain if the face staring back is really him. Or is he still dreaming? Struggling to return to himself, it takes a long time for the trembling to subside.

Leaning on the doorjamb, he gazes back into the darkened bedroom. His long shadow stretches out before him in a rectangle of light from the bathroom. His feet are no longer like bricks. He can move. He reels back to the bed and sits. There's no point in laying down again; trying to fall back into sleep. The night terrors are crushing.

Still gasping, he steps through a door to an outside porch. He's in a cheap motel in a hick town. He's chased The Group-of-Five across the country, but he's certain he's gaining on them. According to the map, there's only one of two places where they can be. He's still troubled that The Senior told him The Haven does not exist when clearly the map shows it does. And the last place on the map, like an extra finger; a peculiar offshoot in the middle of nowhere. The group may have split up. One or two may have gone to the "non-existent" haven. Others to the obscure place, further north. Either way, he has a job to do.

He plops into a plastic basket chair and inhales the sweltering air. Even though it's after midnight, it might as well be high noon as far as the temperature is concerned. He looks up and down the long veranda. Door after door after door to other rooms. No one else stirs. He could be the last man on earth. For now, only a couple of convenience stores across the street shut down for the night. A gas station, a liquor store, a half-dozen scattered houses. But soon it will all change, like so many similar villages, because of climate migrants on the move; ants scrambling over cracked earth.

He thinks about the number of people he's hunted down; dragged back. He wonders if any of the other motel residents are over-aged escapees. And he thinks about all the infusions he's witnessed, cold-heartedly. Always able to walk away unscathed. But he cannot shake William, an intellectually flawed burden on society with nothing to contribute. They had to infuse him for the sake of the cause. They had to. Still, Goodwin cannot shake him.

All the bizarre frustrations aside—*the feet in quicksand*—the dream was reality-based. He *had* witnessed William's infusion. Like so many others, it was via a monitor in another room...

Remote...

Detached.

But William's infusion felt different. Given everything he'd been through, witnessing a gun to his Dadda's head, he still had not lost his gentle sweetness. It was Goodwin who had held him back from Dadda, not the attendant, so he never struggled against him. Even laying on the table with the attendant hovering over him…

"Shh, William… shh…."

…he complied, like a good boy. It wasn't the prick of the needle or the insertion of the hose that baffled him. He simply couldn't understand why Dadda wasn't there.

"Dadda… where's Dadda…?"

Goodwin sits there for a long time, watching the sky slowly brighten on the eastern horizon. Again, he looks up and down the long veranda. Still no one rousing. Yet, he cannot risk it. Pushing up from the basket chair, he steps back into the darkened room, closing the door behind him and shutting out all light, all sound. He thinks about all of it: Each-one-for-Everyone; Eveningsong. None of it has ended his ache.

He lies on the bed and plunges his face into a pillow, unleashing long, anguished, guttural sobs.

***

A vast, cloudless sky…

Stark blue…

From a field stretching all the way to the foothills, Little Robert watches a peregrine circling overhead...

Sasha and Marta spread a blanket in the shade of a trembling aspen, its browning and curling leaves a sign of distress. There wasn't enough snow last winter, so the water table was low. It stunts the wheat.

In the distance, an abandoned oil well, long since dry...

Scattered around it, a half-dozen rusting barrels...

No one takes responsibility for cleaning up the toxicity.

Little Robert makes a sharp crease in a sheet of paper, creating a dart. With a budding pitcher's arm, he sets it soaring, chasing after it as the wind carries it aloft.

Watching from under the tree, Sasha chuckles...

"If he runs any faster, he'll launch."

Marta digs into a cardboard box, taking out three apples and a half-loaf of bread.

"We're awfully low on food..."

Sasha's arrival at his door with Marta, and Little Robert horrified great Uncle Christoff. Even though he has less than a year before Eveningsong, he is unwilling to sacrifice his remaining months in aid of harbouring a grand nephew he barely knows. A bomber, no less. And certainly not a strange woman and her child who are not blood relatives. Terrified that The Administration would descend on him and sentence him to an early infusion, Great Uncle Christoff gave them a meagre box of groceries and sent them packing. So now they're on the road again, doing everything they can to evade The Beige.

It perplexes Sasha that the officer they encountered that night outside the compound let them go. The way she looked at him, he knew she recognized him as the bomber, Sasha Dobrev. She should've made an arrest. All of them, including Little Robert, should be dead by now; infused. As he gazes at the peregrine, soaring above the field, he wonders if the officer is secretly part of the insurgence—the rebellious are everywhere. Why else would she let them go?

As they drove away that night, he'd squinted into the truck's side mirror, seeing the woman silhouetted against the headlights of the police car. He half-expected that at any second she'd change her mind and come after them. But, once over the crest of the hill and at a distance, he knew they were free. As free as a peregrine falcon, settling on the highest branch of the tree. Tucking its wings against its body, it scans the field with an intense glare. Sasha wonders what it makes of Little Robert's paper dart, soaring over the stunted crop.

"Thank you, Robert… Sasha, I mean."

Marta's gentle voice drags him out of his fog.

"For what…?

"For taking such good care of Little Robert and me."

"I've endangered you. If you were smart,

you'd abandon me at the side of the road."

Blushing, Marta lowers her eyes...

"I don't want to be smart."

Looking at her, Sasha knows she's fallen for him; that she's in love. He's in love with her, too. But every single minute they're together endangers her and Little Robert. He should set out across the field right now and never see them again. But as he watches Little Robert shoot the paper dart into the air, he can't bring himself to do it. He wants to spend the rest of his life with them; to take care of them.

He's always been a caretaker. He'd stayed with his feeble parents to the end. His father's weak heart and his mother's emphysema meant an early Eveningsong. Each was a burden on the healthcare system, crumbling like so many other institutions. The Administration allows for the survival of the fittest only. They say they now dedicate all available resources to the sick ecology, previously disregarded. It was at the last minute, and only after the elites realized their personal wealth and power couldn't save them from the choking, stifling air all around the world, and the rancid water, that they acted. Sasha grieves the loss of his father and mother because of hypocrisy; the parents he loved so intensely and admired. His grief made him an angry militant, a bomber, and now a fugitive.

With sudden swiftness, the peregrine swoops from the tree, and snatches up a field mouse. Only a peregrine's piercing eyes could've spotted it in the vastness. It soars to the top of a decaying grain silo, where it tears into the helpless mouse clutched in its talons.

Turning his gaze towards the foothills and the far-off mountains, Sasha remembers the promise he'd made to Marta after Great Uncle Christoff sent them away. He'd get all of them to safety. Somehow.

He unties his neckerchief and spreads it out on the blanket, running his fingers over the intricate pattern, all the way to the bottom corner…

Concentrating…

Decoding.

Marta's voice pulls him back into the real world…

"Are we gonna make it?"

"We have no choice. It's all we have left."

Marta's lips curl into a delicate smile.

"I mean us. Are you and *I* gonna make it…?"

Sasha looks up from the map and takes in her eyes. Deep-seated emotion overwhelms him again. Like it always does when he falls. He slides a finger under her chin and gently draws her face towards him and, for the first time, offers a soft kiss.

From the field, Little Robert beams as he watches his mother and Big Robert under the tree.

He turns his back to the wind and lets out a whoop as he sets free the paper dart. It catches on

the updraft and soars. He chases after it…
Faster…
Faster…
Liftoff.

***

Alistair Goodwin holds up his badge to an elderly man dressed in a tie-dyed caftan. The man looks wary.

"You're out of uniform."

"This badge is my authority. Not the uniform."

He scans the low-slung ranch house with its wide veranda and hanging pots of petunias; its view of the river with the narrow bridge he'd rolled across in his electric.

Peaceful….

Through the roll-up door of the garage, he sees only one vehicle. No doubt it belongs to the man in the caftan.

"I'm here to search your house."

A smirk ripples across the old man's face as he sweeps his hand towards the front door.

"Please. Be my guest."

As he and Goodwin step up onto the porch, the man slips a green blanket off the rail. He then folds it and tosses it onto a nearby rocking chair. They step inside.

Spotless…
Everything in its place…
OC.

Goodwin recalls his room back in the city, his own obsessive-compulsive need for order, control.

The man's voice, casual…

"May I offer you some soup?"

Goodwin breathes in the smell of vegetables in broth.

Salt…

Pepper…

Herbs.

"No time for that."

Again, the man sweeps his hand around the room with a congenial nod.

"Have at it."

Goodwin moves from room to room, taking in everything. Nobody else, anywhere. Again, everything, ship-shape.

He peers into a bathroom. Only one bath towel, one toothbrush, one rinsing glass…

"You live alone?"

"Since my partner's infusion last year."

Sad remembrance permeates the man's dark green eyes.

Quick images flicker through Goodwin's mind's eye. He envisions dinners together at the kitchen table, soup with salt and pepper and herbs. Coffee in bed. He sees matching easy chairs; feet entangled on the ottoman. Crosswords. Chitchat. Laughter. Is this the old man's history, or his own…?

"Melinda…? Nicholas…?"

Goodwin can't suffer the old man's sad green eyes and looks away.

He continues his search, pausing near a bookshelf in the hall, oblivious to the door hidden behind it, the secret room. He runs a finger over a shelf. Not a speck of dust. He knows for certain from the neckerchief map that this place is a Safehouse. But if any of The Group-of-Five ever made it here, they're long gone.

No signs…
No stray hairs…
No fingerprints…
Only ship-shape…
OC.

Later, as Goodwin drives back over the narrow bridge and along the local road to the highway, he's convinced that, recently, The Group-of-Five were there. The place was a little too swept and polished. The old man had ensured there were no traces in that house of anyone other than him. And there's something else roiling in his detecting gut. Something about the green blanket. Why would the old man even think of removing it from the porch rail while ushering one of The Beige into his house for a search? It was more than OC. Maybe the green blanket is one of those minute details that'll make sense later. Like the neckerchief did. Only after unwittingly viewing it repeatedly on the security cam footage after the bombing in Coal Town did it become relevant. Only then did it become apparent it was a map. So, for now, he places the green blanket in the back of his mind. Like always, he'll let his subconscious work it out.

As he drives through the foothills and deeper into the mountains, they appear to shapeshift. What was flat and purple from afar become alive as he nears them. The sun creates shadows in crevices and reflects a panoply of colours from the minerals streaked through their chiseled facets. But the snow-caps are shrinking. Almost disappeared. There are thick forests, although dying. As a child, he'd camped in the mountains with his parents. He remembers there being more wildlife. Now, beyond a flitting bird or two, it appears scarce. This surprises him.

He's read dozens of reports from The Administration about recovery; about how all their policies are working. The reports assure that, although the ecology came close to the tipping point, cooperating nations have averted it. The laws of Each-One-For-Everyone and Eveningsong work. Reducing the population with death at sixty has saved everyone. But as he drives along the highway, taking it all in, none of it coincides.

High on the mountainsides, there are bald patches. Back in the day, loggers clear-cut everything. Tree planters tried to restore the areas, but even from afar, the saplings appear brown. And there are other areas where lightning strikes cause forest fires, which burn them out.

After parsing the neckerchief map, he turns off the main highway onto an abandoned logging road, twisting this way and that between two steep mountains.

He travels deeper...

Deeper still.

Soon, looming cliffs create a narrow corridor. Tunnel-like...

Shadowed...

Dark...

All-embracing.

He keeps going. God help him if the battery in his electric dies.

Finally, he emerges from the passage into a sunlit canyon, arriving at a fork in the road.

CHAPTER 14

Elizabeth, drifting...
Effects from an infusion.
Images...
Remembrance...

She, at four or five, running across a field with a buttercup she discovered. Father, lifting her up and swinging her around. Telling her about how there were so many more buttercups when he was a boy. And cornflowers and daisies too. Oh, so many more.

She, at ten or twelve, the sun beating down, hot and dry. Feeling sticky from a thick coat of sunscreen, Mother rubs into her skin to protect her from damaging rays. She contemplates a fish in the pond out back. Mother tells her there were so many more back in the day.

She, at sixteen or seventeen. Conversations with father. Nature has lost its balance; is falling apart. We didn't act fast enough. We should've done more to stop it.

Drifting...
The law of Each-One-For-Everyone...

Eveningsong...

Sacrifice for the good of all.

The Administration comes down hard. They have no choice. They say everyone must make sacrifices. Goodbye, grandma. Goodbye, grandpa. Thank you for dying to save me. I promise I'll do the same for my children's children.

Rich and poor...

Even those controlling the levers of power are doing their bit, they say.

It's a lie.

Drifting...

Father figures it out. Knows too much. Shot dead in the street.

Drifting...

Elizabeth, embittered, becomes an avenging angel.

The planning...

The subterfuge...

Falsifying her identity and worming her way into a job with The Administration as a low-level functionary. But one with genius. She has more power than any of the superiors' suspects. With access to the grey matter within the system's brain, she unravels it; bends it to her will.

Drifting...

Elizabeth, standing on a promontory overlooking The Haven...

Through her binoculars, she sees The Beige seize an unsuspecting man who arrives at the gates. He looks confused, in a daze. He believes this is a place of refuge. But The Haven is not for the likes of him. He doesn't belong. He lashes out, trying to escape them. But they overpower him. They drag him inside an impressive wooden building, painted white. They strap him to a table and force an infusion. Like hundreds of others who arrive here, The Haven is not their sanctuary. The Amphorium, with its smoky chimney and the smell of incineration, is their last stop. It's a trap.

Elizabeth records all of it on her cell phone, narrating as a half-dozen of The Beige scramble up the slope towards her...

"They're upon me. They'll shoot me now or infuse me, but you've seen everything...."

She presses SEND....

Drifting...

Elizabeth, captured...

Hands bound behind her back...

Imposing wrought-iron gates closing behind her.

A contingent of The Beige prods her forward along a wide boulevard lined with small but lavish houses.

Abundant gardens...

Lush...

Green...

Rare flowers and plants unseen in a long time...

It's everything she expects...

Each detail her father revealed to her before they shot him dead.

From their verandas, people eye her up and down as she passes. Each one of them is ancient, verging on decrepitude. Well beyond Eveningsong. She recognizes all of them as the upper echelon of former Administrations. Outraged, they glare at her, fearing what will befall them because of her.

Lifting her gaze, she sees the most beautiful of all the houses, jutting out of a high slope.

Prismatic…

Hanging gardens…

Wide terraces with a panoramic view.

The Beige lead her up a zigzagging path to the house, and to a stooped, but imposing man standing on a terrace, gazing out over everything. He's the charismatic leader of the powerful, the entitled, the downright evil. Of all the fat cats, he's the fattest.

His face, jowly…

Leathery skin, sagging…

Bleached hair vainly combed over his balding pate…

A fine suit hangs awkwardly on his bulbous body.

Silently, he keeps his back to Elizabeth, her presence unacknowledged. Finally, after interminable silence, he speaks; his voice is a sneering wheeze.

"Elizabeth Lowell. Member of the notorious Group-of-Five…."

Reaching out, he takes Elizabeth's cell phone from one of The Beige.

He turns to face her. "What have you done?"

She has exposed him and the others in this place for what they are. Liars and hypocrites who believe the rules do not apply to them. Only to those they consider common. But thanks to Elizabeth, the masses, who have sacrificed so much, have now lost their blinders. They're livid. Thanks to her, they've discovered the secret mountain pass and, even now, their rageful drums echo in the canyon.

Rrrrrum-tum-tium...

They've made the drums their emblem.

Ta-tum, ta-tum, ta-tum...

The end to mendacity. They're coming.

Finally, Elizabeth can let go. She's done what she set out to do.

Now buttercups, cornflowers, daisies.

Hello grandma...

Hello grandpa...

Hello father.

Drifting...

Drifting...

Gone.

***

Rampage...

It was bound to happen. The Senior watches his wall of screens, horrified. Elizabeth Lowell has done her worst. Video broadcasts repeatedly across all platforms. The Administration is powerless to stop it. From a vantage point high above The Haven, she has exposed the savagery, the self-serving hypocrisy, clear to anyone who sees it. How did she manage it? It's her genius.

And so, riots from village to city. Even now, The Senior hears bangs at the entry to the administration building. And the drums. The incessant drums...

Ta-tum, ta-tum.

Days ago, he had a sick feeling in the pit of his gut. He should've followed his instincts; told Cherise to pack up the girls and prepare to leave. But he never expected this. He prays to God they're safe. Somewhere.

He watches the monitors, all rebroadcasting the same images, unchecked; a half-dozen of The Beige scales a slope towards Elizabeth Lowell. It must be her, narrating everything. He recognizes her voice...

"They're upon me. They'll shoot me now or infuse me, but you've seen everything...."

"What's she using to broadcast? A cell phone?"

One of The Beige reaches her. The butt of his rifle appears to jump out of the screen. All the monitors go black. Then the cycle begins again. Over and over. Unstoppable.

Again, The Senior hears the bangs at the doors...

Louder...

Louder.

The drums. The persistent drums...

Ta-tum, ta tum.

He steps from his office, his mouth agape.

Workers from the colour-coded pods brush past him, knocking against him as they flee toward the back of the building. The Beige stand at the ready, their pistols trained on the entry doors, which weaken from the force of a battering ram.

"What are they using...?"

The Beige will meet them with bullets. But they know they're outnumbered. One young officer presses his lips together, tasting salty sweat dripping from his forehead and down his cheeks.

Frantic, The Senior punches numbers on his cell phone. Cherise still isn't picking up. He envisions her phone shattered on the ground somewhere. She and the girls, taken.

It's happening quickly. All the pent-up anger. The suspicion. Losing faith. History repeating itself. Anarchy.

It isn't supposed to end this way. As a Senior in The Administration, they guaranteed him a quiet retirement in The Haven; a privileged one if he could keep the secret. It's his right. He's done everything he's supposed to do for the cause; followed the rules. It's his right.

The doors bulge...

Splinter.

Officers look over their shoulders towards him. They need guidance, direction. He points at three of them...

"You, you, and you. Up to the roof. Fire into

the crowd. They'll retreat...."

He needs reinforcements. He quick dials his cell phone. At the other end, the line rings and rings and rings. No one picks up.

Something has broken loose. For years, The Administration had it all under control; had all of *them* under control. No more. Elizabeth Lowell has exposed the lie, the sham.

The doors give way, and a jeep crashes through. It spins into one of The Beige, who can't move away fast enough.

The angry mob floods in, brandishing rudimentary weapons: sticks, rocks; ready to die. The Beige fire on them, but they're soon overwhelmed.

Stones...

Clubs...

Beatings.

Someone in the mob sees the impressive badge pinned to The Senior's chest, and shouts...

The Senior draws his pistol and fires into the onslaught.

Two men fall.

But soon, others overwhelm him, throw him to the floor...

Punches...

Kicks...

Ringing in his ears...

The tangy taste of blood in his mouth.

***

Jack, by the lake, looking skyward…

A thousand feet above the secluded valley, fighter jets rocket across the sky, west to east. The roar is deafening. It takes a long time before the sound trails off, before a return to silence. Peace. Something's happening beyond the mountains. Whatever it is, Jack hopes it will never find its way to this place…this Eden.

Startled by the sound, Little Robert also looks up. He stands in the shallows of the lakeshore with his pant legs rolled up to his knees. Once the jets have all but disappeared, becoming dots in the sky, he returns to a more important task, chasing after a tiny frog jumping from rock to rock.

Two days ago, Sasha Dobrev had stumbled, half-starved, out of the bush with the boy and his mother in tow. His relief was palpable. He had not misread the map. He'd found the way and led them to a place that's safe for now; to a porch where he can sit with Marta and watch Little Robert chase a frog. For the time being, he won't think about jets, or where they're headed, and why.

After squinting into the sun and to the disappearing aircraft, Yelena returns to her weeding. The vegetables in the garden patch are surviving well. They must. The chickens and the goats must survive. And the scant fish in the warming lake must survive, and the trees. And all of them; this newfound family must endure.

There's no news of Elizabeth Lowell. Hope is that one day she'll find her way along the hidden path and emerge from the forest. Henry believes it's unlikely. Her mission was more about sacrifice than survival. Watching the dissipating vapor trailing the jets, Henry wonders if her sacrifice has anything to do with what's happening in the outside world.

***

Penitence....
Alistair Goodwin is delirious, weak from hunger. He has a miserable fever he doesn't understand, and he's nauseous. He must've picked up a bug somewhere. A sick stomach only compounds his feelings of hopelessness.

He's been stumbling through the bush for hours; ever since he left his electric where the road ended and the dense forest began. Even if he abandons his mission and turns back, there's no point. The battery in the electric is dead. He has no choice but to push forward. It's been a while since he's run across a tree with a notch carved into it, and he wonders if he's veered off the path. He feels on the verge of collapse. If he doesn't find the way soon, he's done for.

Before the battery went dead in the electric, he saw one last news flash on his screen: riots everywhere. All hell is breaking loose.

Contrition....
(An inner voice keeps whispering words to

him.)

He steps into a small glade and examines the neckerchief map. Which way is North? Squinting through the dappled dimness, he scans one tree after another. Finally, he sees it. A notch.

Amends....

He follows an obscure path, hoping beyond all else that it leads to a lake in a hidden valley deep in the mountains. If the map is correct, he should be close. He sends up a prayer to a God he doesn't believe in that when he arrives, someone is there. If not, it's over.

Then he hears it. A man's voice, deep, resonant. And then another, responding.

Brushing aside a branch, he peers out from behind a bush. He's astonished by what he sees: a cabin with solar panels and a wind turbine. A garden patch, chickens and goats. Seated on the porch, Sasha Dobrev, and a woman he has never seen before. A young boy leaps about, dodging this way and that, in a game that makes sense only to him. Most surprising of all, Yelena Chomsky. She's alive. And the voices he hears are those of Jack Parnell and Henry Chagall; the two men whom he seeks above all others. Standing by the lake, they're in deep conversation. He cocks an ear, but he cannot make out their words. He senses their overwhelming grief; the grief for which he is responsible.

Or is the grief he senses his own...?

"Melinda... Nicholas."

He envisions the great tidal wave sweeping through the narrow streets between high-rise buildings, bursting the windows. His wife and son, unable to escape, overwhelmed. Drowned.

"Heartache...."

(The inner voice again.)

He has not come to capture anybody; to take them back. Especially Jack Parnell and Henry Chagall. No. He must make them understand he has come for another purpose.

Atonement....

He watches the young boy, captivated by everything he sees: leaves, bugs, caterpillars. He dashes here and there, intensely focused on one thing, and then soon distracted by another. The boy is about the same age as Nicholas was when he died, the memory of him forever stamped in Alistair's mind. He could well be him. Or is it delirium that makes it seem so? The sick stomach. Watching the boy sprint here and there, he feels overwhelming sorrow.

If he reveals himself; if he were to step from the bush right now, would they believe him? Forgive him? He's not here to confront them, capture them for infusion. No. He's come for a singular reason. To make amends for the child in a man's body...

"William...."

(The inner voice...)

"Oh, my Melinda...my Nicholas...."

He wells up inside and tears trickle down his

cheek.

All the death. All the destruction. And him, a part of it. They needn't accept his apology. Their pain may be too great. But he must say it, say the words. He must. Then he can rest. He'll wander into the bush and let nature take its course. He must believe in an afterlife. To see Melinda and Nicholas again, he must. It'll allow him to let go.

Drawing nearer, he slumps to the ground, the fever overwhelming him. He can now make out the words as Jack Parnell speaks to Henry Chagall…

"I had a dream, Henry."

"Of course you did, my love. It's another way you overthink."

"I dreamed there are no longer witnesses.

Everyone with their history is long gone; our stories, lost.

There are no eyes left to see the desiccated earth.

No breathable air. Only suffocation.

All the water has evaporated.

Only the remains of crumbling buildings, useless edifices.

There is no one to kneel before rugged crosses or other emblems prostrating before God.

Any God.

No wars. No one left to march into battle for any conviction whatsoever.

Neither fortune nor empires.

The thirst for power…bloodlust. All taken.

All of it, a ruin. Inhospitable for anything animate.

Only stones. Only dust, and no air to stir it. Just silence. Tranquillity.

The planet did not need us. It took us out; saved itself.

I dreamed there are no eyes to see a hopeful seed resting in the shade of a rock.

It waits for a shift in the universe, the return of rain.

Only then will it crack and sprout, begin the long journey back.

It'll take millennia, if ever.

But until then, there are no eyes to rocket into space.

To look back at a lifeless planet, once blue, now brown, suspended in the black...

Spinning...
Spinning...
Spinning."

***

Later, Jack stands alone by the lakeshore, letting the breeze drift over his skin. He thinks about the ashes that he and Henry spread amongst the wildflowers at the ramshackle farm. If they were not Yelena's, then whose were they? The ashes of someone who has no one to claim them; no one left to love them; grieve their loss.

A sudden and thunderous crack startles him out of his maudlin thoughts. The entire rock face at the north end of the valley gives way and collapses with a horrific roar. Enormous boulders plunge into the lake, sending out ripples that multiply into a tsunami, rolling across the lake. Stunned, Jack stands frozen in its path.

From the cabin's porch, Henry calls out to him…

"Jack! Jack…!"

Transfixed, Jack seems not to hear.

Others rush out from the cabin as Henry bolts from the porch.

"Jack…!"

But the terrible tide sweeps ashore, overwhelming Jack. Then receding, it claws him into the churn: tossing him, turning him.

Alistair Goodwin darts from the bush and dives into the water. Although fevered and sick, adrenaline kicks in, and he acts out of instinct. With all his strength, he swims through the swirl, finally reaching Jack, who thrashes hopelessly disoriented, ingesting gulps of water.

Goodwin grabs him by the collar and struggles against the outgoing tide, back towards the shore. By then, Henry reaches them, and Sasha also wades into the receding tide. Together they drag Jack and Goodwin, coughing, choking, back onto dry land.

Stretched out in the mud and gasping for air, Goodwin looks over at Jack, laying beside him, spitting up water. Then he looks up at Henry, Yelena, Sasha, and Marta, all gathered around him,

blinking, stunned. And the boy...
Everything goes black.

***

Little Robert sits on a log contemplating a fuzzy caterpillar, inching its way to somewhere important. He looks up the slope towards the cabin. It's home now. His mother and Big Robert linger on the porch with the others: a woman named Yelena, and two men named Henry and Jack. They say they're all family now. And they tell Little Robert that they're his family now too. Thinking about it makes him feel squishy inside.

Safe.

The other man is there too. The one who came out of nowhere and saved Jack from drowning. They call him Goodwin. His fever has broken, and his strength is returning. Little Robert has seen him, slump-shouldered, in conversation with Henry and Jack. And he has seen Jack and Henry, their heads bowed, nod and proffer their hand. It's all too complicated to understand, but Little Robert figures it's a good thing.

Everyone seems worried about what is happening beyond the mountains. And here too. Yelena keeps a constant eye on the garden patch, watering it, and nurturing the plants. Even though the lake almost took Jack, each day he stands in its shallows taking its temperature and looking for fish, counting them. Henry, Big Robert, and Goodwin labour to expand the cabin. Mother scrubs and cooks and teaches him stuff like words and numbers. And tells him stories. She smiles at Big Robert every chance she gets. Then blushes when he smiles back.

From time to time, Little Robert overhears conversations on the porch about chain reactions and about the collapse of the rock cliff and the big wave; about how none of this is the way things are supposed to be. And none of it's the way things used to be. They talk about how everything relies on everything else to survive. And they wonder if it will.

Are they talking about the earth? Are they talking about him?

Yesterday, Little Robert saw a sparrow flit past. Jack told him it's needed somewhere, and that the flutter of its wings may cause a ripple effect that will save the world.

Manufactured by Amazon.ca
Bolton, ON